PENGUIN BOOKS

TALES
FROM
THE
HINTERLAND

ALSO BY MELISSA ALBERT

THE HAZEL WOOD
THE NIGHT COUNTRY

TALES
FROM
THE
HINTERLAND

MELISSA ALBERT

ILLUSTRATED BY NICK HAYES

PENGUIN BOOKS

PENGUIN BOOKS

UK | USA | Canada | Ireland | Australia
India | New Zealand | South Africa

Penguin Books is part of the Penguin Random House group of companies
whose addresses can be found at global.penguinrandomhouse.com.

www.penguin.co.uk
www.puffin.co.uk
www.ladybird.co.uk

First published in the USA by Flatiron Books
and in Great Britain by Penguin Books 2021

001

Text copyright © Melissa Albert, 2021
Illustrations copyright © Nick Hayes, 2021

The moral right of the author and illustrator has been asserted

Printed and bound in Great Britain by Clays Ltd, Elcograf S.p.A.

A CIP catalogue record for this book is available from the British Library

ISBN: 978–0–241–37189–3

All correspondence to:
Penguin Books
Penguin Random House Children's
One Embassy Gardens, 8 Viaduct Gardens
London SW11 7BW

To all the readers whose first language was fairy tales

TALES
FROM THE
HINTERLAND

BY
ALTHEA
PROSERPINE

COLLECTED BY
MELISSA ALBERT

THE
DOOR
THAT
WASN'T
THERE

There was once a rich merchant who lived at the edge of the woods, in a tiny town in the Hinterland. Though he spent most of his days traveling, he was at home long enough to give his wife two daughters, the eldest dark and the youngest golden, born one year apart.

Their father was distant and their mother was strange, often shutting herself up in her room for hours. Her daughters could hear her speaking to someone when they pressed their ears to the door, but only the eldest, Anya, ever made out an answer. The voice she heard was so thin and rustling, she could almost believe it was leaves against the window.

On a winter's day when Anya was sixteen, their mother locked her door and did not open it again. After three days the servants broke it down, and found—an empty room. The windows were shut, winter howled outside, and the woman was gone. But she'd left something behind: on the floor, in a puddle of blood, a bone dagger.

Anya heard the servants whispering about it and crept into the room to see for herself. The stain she found on the floor infected her with a horror of blood so fearsome, she took to washing out her monthly rags in the dark.

The servants sent word to the girls' father that his wife was dead, or gone, or worse, and for a time heard no reply. Until the first warm day of spring, when he drove up to the house in an unfamiliar carriage.

Inside it was the girls' new mother. In silken slippers, clinging to their father's arm, she stepped out onto the cobblestones. She was smaller than Anya, with a heap of pale hair and blue eyes that switched coldly from one stepdaughter to the next.

For half a year their father stayed home, besotted with his new wife and tolerating his children. They ran as wild as they always had, accustomed by then to raising themselves, and thought very little of their new stepmother.

But their father grew bored of the woman in the end, as he'd once grown bored of their mother—as he'd always been bored of his daughters. On that day, he kissed his new wife goodbye, nodded at his daughters, and was gone.

Now their stepmother had the run of the house, and of her stepdaughters. Whether she was bored or whether she was wicked, it came out to the same thing in the end. First she snapped at the girls, demanding they stay close by her. Then she pushed them away, slapping them at the slightest provocation, carrying scissors in her pocket to cut off hanks of their long hair. When she left the house, she locked them up—to keep them from misbehaving, she said. But she kept them in their mother's room, where the windows were warped shut and the stain on the floor taunted Anya like a vile black mouth. Their mother's bed had been chopped into firewood after her disappearance, all the pretty objects she'd surrounded herself with sold or locked away. The girls rattled like seeds around the empty room, avoiding the poisonous blot on the floor.

At first their stepmother stayed away for a few hours. Then whole days, then entire nights. The first time she left them locked up from dusk to the next, Anya beat on the door and screamed until her throat and fists were raw, but no one came.

When the stepmother finally opened the door, she wrinkled her nose at the smell and gestured at the chamber pot. "Empty it," she said. Kohl and rouge melted into candy swirls on her cheeks; she wouldn't meet her stepdaughters' eyes.

There came a day when she locked them in with a bowl of apples and a jug of water and did not come back. The sun rose and fell, rose and fell. On the third day Anya looked out the window and saw the servants walking down the lane, their belongings on their backs.

The house was empty. The apples were eaten, the water long gone. The window wouldn't open and the glass wouldn't shatter, even when Anya smashed at it with her boot.

That night the sisters lay together in the middle of the floor, trying to keep each other warm. Lisbet was sunk in shallow sleep when Anya heard a sound she'd nearly forgotten. A sound like leaves rustling together outside an unlatched window.

It came from the bloodstain on the floor. Slowly she inched her way toward it, resting her ear just over it and holding her breath. It was deep, deep in the night when the rustling resolved into a voice.

You will die, the voice told her.

Anya rolled away, angry. *I know,* she replied fiercely, in her mind. *We're half-dead already.*

You will die, the voice said again. *Unless.*

And it told her how she could save herself and her sister. How she could remake the world just enough so that they could live.

It would take blood.

When the sun rose Anya told Lisbet what she'd learned. Their mother wasn't dead, she was gone. She'd used magic to make a door, and it had taken her far, far away. Their mother's blood had spoken to Anya, and told her how to make a door of their own.

"It will take blood," she told Lisbet, "but it can't be mine."

This was a lie. Anya wasn't cruel, she was frightened. The idea of opening her own veins filled her with a terror that felt like falling, forward and forward without end. She swallowed the bitter taste of the lie and took the bone knife from the place the voice told her she'd find it: behind a loose brick inside the fireplace.

"The blood can't be mine," she said again, "because I'm the sorcerer. I must make the door, and you must sacrifice the blood for it."

Lisbet nodded, but something in her eyes told Anya she knew the words were a lie.

This made her angry. When she drew the blade

across her sister's wrist, the anger made her careless, and the blade bit too deep.

Lisbet said nothing as her sister took her wrist and used it to paint a door.

She painted the sides of it first, in two continuous lines, scraping Lisbet's wrist over the stone. She lifted the girl as high as she could to paint a lintel over the top. When Anya eased her back onto her feet, Lisbet was as white as the flesh of an apple.

Anya turned away from her sister's drained face and said the words that would make the blood into a door. Words the voice had said into her ear, three times so she'd remember.

All at once the stone wicked up the blood, and the red of it became lines of warm white light. The newly made door swung toward them, letting out a breath of warm air and a scent like clean cotton. They held hands and watched it open.

Then Lisbet moaned, and swayed, and crumpled to the ground. Her arm stretched out, her cold fingertips nearly touching the door.

The door that wasn't there, and then was. The door that her lifeblood fed.

At the moment she let go her last breath, the white light shuddered and went green. The green of infected wounds, of nightmares, of the rind of mold that crawled over week-old bread. The cotton scent turned dusty and stuck in Anya's throat. She threw herself against the door, but it was too late. It opened, inch by inch, yawning with dank air like the mouth of a cellar.

Anya didn't think her mother could be behind that door, but she had nowhere else to go. She lifted Lisbet and carried her through.

The room she stepped into was just like the one they'd left, but reversed. Anya's eye went to where the stain on the floor should be. In its place was a pool of bright blood, freshly shed. She limped across the room, still holding her sister's body, and wrenched open the door.

The hall behind it curved left instead of right, and the lanterns on the wall were gone, replaced with paintings of people Anya didn't recognize. Their eyes were charred holes and their mouths were wet and red. The hall hummed with heavy green light.

Cradling Lisbet, Anya moved through the house. It was cold and smelled of coal dust and iron. In every fireplace curled heatless flames. On every table were plates of rotting meat, or glossy dark flowers with pollen dripping livid from their hearts.

When she opened the front door she saw the sickness spread beyond the house. The branches of trees had become slender bones, the dust of the road crackling ashes.

I did this, she said to herself. *I killed my sister—her death made a door, and the door opened onto death!*

It took hours, but she dug deeply enough into the burnt earth to bury her sister. Then she set off toward town, to see if she could find anything living.

Town was a place of strange horrors. Not a body to

be seen, human nor animal, just a heavy sky that bathed the whole world in light the color of disease, and locked houses, and windows painted a blind black.

Anya grieved and wandered but never wearied. She needed neither sleep nor food nor drink, and when she ran the bone knife over her own wrist it made no nick in her skin. In desperation she scaled the vines spilling over the walls of a cottage, hoisting herself onto the crumbling gray shingles of its roof. From there, she jumped.

She drifted to earth like an autumn leaf, touching down unharmed. There she lay, praying for an end, though every prayer tasted as bitter as the lie that had killed her sister.

It was then that the voice spoke to her once more.

It had been a long time since she'd lain on the floor of her mother's bedroom letting it whisper secrets into her ear. Longer than she thought. Far away, her stepmother was dead, killed by a fever. Her father had taken a new bride, who'd borne him a son.

Will you take me back home? Anya pleaded.

You're asking the wrong question, the voice replied.

It led her through town, back to the grave she'd dug in front of her father's house. From it a black walnut tree had grown. Its rustling leaves were the only moving things in the blighted land. "Lisbet," Anya said, and laid her hand on its trunk.

With a rustle like a sigh, the tree dropped three walnuts into her hands. She cracked them open one by one.

The first held a satin dress the color of moth's wings.

The second held a pair of slippers with the black shine of petrified wood.

The third held a translucent stone the size of an eye.

When she peered through the stone, the world around her burst into life. The day was clear, the trees were blooming, and a carriage was bearing down on her. The driver didn't see her, but the horse did, and reared, hooves high over Anya's head.

She dropped the stone, returning to her miserable realm. Now she understood what her sister had given her: a window onto the land of the living.

Do with it what you will, the voice told her, *but do not squander your sister's gifts.*

Anya waited until the green light had faded to murk, marking night in this in-between place. She put on the moth-wing dress and the slippers. She combed back her heavy hair. Then she raised the stone to her eye.

She saw her home as she once knew it, when she was a girl with a mother and a father and a sister named Lisbet. She held the stone in place like a peephole, circling the house and looking into its windows.

In one candlelit room she saw a beautiful woman playing the piano. Her father drinking a glass of sherry, his hair lined with gray. And a boy just older than her. He was tall and narrow, growing into manhood but not yet there.

Anya's father looked at him proudly, clapping a hand to his shoulder. The boy's gaze roved idly over the room, and his mother at the piano, before landing on Anya.

Frowning, he moved to the window. Anya shrank back as her father joined his son. The boy pointed, but their father looked past her, shaking his head. Finally he pulled the curtains closed.

Anya waited in the garden, in her dress the color of will-o'-the-wisps. When she lowered her arm, she stood in a place of rotting bowers and bone. When she raised the stone back to her eye, she could see the soft grass and the brief starlight of fireflies. She could see the boy walking toward her, his step tentative but his face eager.

"You may ask me one question," she told him. "But it has to be the right one."

"Who are you?" he asked.

Anya said nothing.

"Why can't they see you?" he pleaded.

She stayed silent.

"You are very beautiful," he whispered, reaching out to touch her. "Why do you hold your hand so high?"

Anya smiled at him the way she'd once seen her stepmother smile at her father. She let him bend close to her mouth, closer, before dropping her arm and returning to the dead garden.

It took her father's son many nighttime meetings to ask the right question. By then his eyes were hollow with sleeplessness, and he looked at her with a love like hunger.

"How can I get you to stay?" he asked at last.

She smiled and put her mouth to his ear.

She told him how they could be together. How he

could remake the world just enough so she could stand beside him.

It would take blood.

She taught him the words to say, repeating them three times so he would remember. She pressed her bone knife into his hand. And she watched as he slid his bleeding wrist over the wall of her father's house, using it to paint a door. He swayed as he spoke the words, his face, a mirror of their father's, going pale.

The blood turned into a door that glowed with wicked green light at the seams. Anya dropped the stone from her eye as it swung open.

The boy disappeared, and the light turned into the warm golden lamplight of home. As Anya walked through the door, she could feel the faintest brush of her half-brother, stepping past her into the lifeless place that death had made.

Then she was standing in her father's house, alive and alone, and Death didn't feel cheated because she'd traded him one prisoner for another. She lifted the stone just long enough to peep through it at the boy standing in her place, his face terrified, before putting it into her pocket.

She went to the kitchen and ate spoonfuls of honey, wolfed up fistfuls of meat, let wine run down her chin. Then she climbed the stairs to her father's bedroom, where he lay sleeping next to his wife. She felt the bone knife she'd snatched back from the lost boy twitching where it lay against her breast.

She didn't cut her father's throat. She cut his wife's.

She laid the stone in the dead woman's hand, where her father would be sure to find it. And hold it to his eye, to see the dead world that crouched beside his own, and the son who would call to him, always, but whom he could never retrieve.

HANSA
THE
TRAVELER

There was a girl who spoke to the moon. That isn't enough to make a tale, but to her the moon spoke back.

The girl's name was Hansa, and she lived with her grandmother an hour's walk from the sea. Her father was a ship's captain who came home every year or so, filled their cottage for a time with his tales and laughter, grew restless, and slipped away again.

When he was home he took Hansa walking through the raggedy town that grew up around the harbor. From the port she watched the water smooth into glass and purl into lace and worry itself into great waves beyond the cove. There were things to see on shore, too: a witch who made good-luck charms out of the hair of drowned men. A tinker with a blue eye and a green, so you knew one of the two was fairy-kissed but you didn't know which. The salt-stained atlas her father bought for her, whose pictures moved of their own accord.

But he always delivered her back to their cottage and her grandmother before dark. Because, while Hansa had seen many things and imagined many more, there was one she couldn't conceive of: Hansa had never seen the night.

Every evening as the sun lowered itself, her grandmother latched the doors and windows and drew the curtains tight. She made Hansa sit beside her till bedtime, unsnarling her knitting. On the nights Hansa's sight went blurry with boredom and the whole onion-scented cottage seemed tight as a fist, she dreamed furious dreams of running away, as her father had, to sea. Perhaps her grandmother knew of these dreams, because she kept Hansa's world as small as she could, bordered by their cottage walls and punctuated by chaperoned walks in the sun. "Children do not go out at night," she said through tight lips, when Hansa pressed her on the subject. As her father had told her no differently, Hansa had no choice but to believe it.

Years passed before she learned, from the butcher's boy, that not all children are kept from the night. Twelve years old and flushed with fury, she demanded an explanation.

"Is it wolves I have to fear?" she asked. "Highway robbers with stolen brides? Dead women with pointed teeth?"

"None of those," said her grandmother, who had no imagination. She sighed and set down her knitting. "What you must fear is the Moon. I had it from your father the day he brought you home to me: the Moon will kill you as soon as look at you, and you must be kept from her sight."

This was very interesting to Hansa. More than anything she wanted to know how she'd made such an enemy of this stranger, the Moon. She thought long on how she might escape her grandmother's watchful eye, settling at last on a plan: she would, each night, serve the old woman tea with white honey, mixing it sweeter and sweeter until the honey could hide the flavor of the herb that cured sleeplessness.

On that night Hansa steeped the herb in the syrupy tea. She kept her face turned toward the fire as her grandmother drank it down. The old woman nodded her head, slowly, slowly, until it dropped to her chest and she was sleeping.

The moment her eyes blinked shut, a wind came down the chimney. It swept past Hansa and set all the curtains in the house to twitching. One moved aside just long enough for Hansa to spy something through it: a bright button pinned to the night sky like a medal to a general's chest.

So this was the Moon, her enemy. Though Hansa had never seen her before, she recognized her at once: she knew the Sun had a sister, and a whole host of nieces that sugared the sky at night. Hansa ran to her room, peeled back the curtain, and used one of her grandmother's knitting needles to pick the lock on her window.

Night air poured over the sill. It reached in like a hand with starry rings on every finger and scooped her up. She lay on the roof in her nightgown, gazing at the Moon and her daughters. Though she was not unafraid, she was the happiest she'd ever been.

Hello, Moon, she said in her mind. *Why is it I must fear you?*

Hello, granddaughter, the Moon replied. *There is no need for fear. Indeed, I am your greatest friend.*

Hansa was not surprised. In the endless, unfamiliar

realm of night, it felt natural that the Moon should speak to her.

My grandmother is asleep downstairs, she said drowsily, without opening her mouth. *Why do you call me grand-daughter?*

Your father's mother sleeps inside, said the Moon, *but I am the mother of your mother, and now is not my time to rest.*

Hansa's heart quickened. Nobody ever spoke of her mother, not even to curse her for her absence. Hansa had always felt as motherless as a tree.

But even a tree has roots, said the Moon. *And the seed that births it. You're young still, but old enough. If you'll listen, I'll tell you a tale of your mother.*

It was a moonless night when your parents met, a night so calm and clear that the Stars, my daughters, could see themselves in the water. Because your mother is vain as a mermaid, she drew too close to the sea. Your father was looking into the water when he saw her face reflected over his shoulder. Her beauty was such that he caught her by a hand, and he caught her by a heel, and he pulled her onto his ship.

If I'd been close I would have stunned him with my light and sent him to the sea wolves. But the night was moonless, as I said, so he and my daughter had their foolish way with each other.

It was another such night, when he was homeward bound, that she stepped onto his deck and gave him a child wrapped in a blanket woven of storm clouds, bits of thunder trapped in its folds to soothe the little one's sleep.

"Hide her from the night," your mother told him, for it was you wrapped in that blanket. "Hide her from the Moon. If my mother learns of her, she'll tell my husband of our congress. He's a Tide, and in his jealousy will drown you both."

Stars do not make good parents, nor do they make good wives, but your mother was trying to protect you. And sailors make their living by the tides, so your father was too fearful of their betrayal to risk your ever being seen. Foolish daughter, foolish man: I would no more give up a baby to a jealous Tide than rise in the morning. But Stars cannot keep a secret, and I learned of you soon enough. Long have I watched for you, long have I waited to tell you this tale.

Now, the Moon said. Now that you're grown, and able, I must ask something of you.

Am I grown? Hansa asked. Her mind's mirror was silvered over with storm clouds and sea voyages and tides.

You're grown enough. Now I'll tell you of the night another Star, silliest of my daughters, told your mother's husband of her indiscretion. His rage roiled the seabed. It lifted shipwrecks and their ghosts and sent them sailing. It tilted the pan of the sky. The jealous Tide dragged your mother from her constellation and took her to the rim of the world.

She lives there still, his captive. I do not know the form of her imprisonment, for even the Moon cannot see what lies at the rim of the world. Will you go to her? Will you set her free?

The sea, Hansa thought. The way to the world's rim lies by sea. She thought of the broken glitter the sea made of the sun's light, and imagined what it might do with the coolness of the moon. It would, perhaps, make a road she could walk upon.

Not quite, the Moon said, sounding amused. *You'll go by ship.*

She tilted her head over the girl and cried three tears. They shone in her lap like hard white eyes as the Moon gave her instructions:

Pack what you must and go to the harbor.

Ignore the first merchant who approaches you. Bow to the second. To the third, offer one of my tears in exchange for whatever they'll give you.

Find a ship with a maiden's name, and trade a second tear for passage.

Then the Moon gave her a cold kiss. All that night Hansa slept with her window open, in a pool of her grandmother's light. When she woke between moonset and sunrise, three tears lay in her hand, and the Moon's instructions were fresh in her head.

She rose and packed her cloak, a loaf of bread, two books, and the Moon's three tears. She crept past her father's mother, still asleep before the cold hearth, and slipped out into the day. When she reached the harbor, the first merchant to approach her was a man in shabby clothes, selling all manner of charms: dried seeds he called serpents' tongues, a string of stones he claimed were the Moon's own tears, which Hansa would've known for river pearls even if she hadn't the proof of his lies in her pocket. She passed him without a look.

The second merchant was a green-dressed woman,

very tall, whose one eye watched Hansa carefully. Hansa bowed to her deeply, and the lady seemed satisfied.

The third merchant was a girl of about fifteen, who informed Hansa cheerfully that her mother had a taste for drink and for sailors, and all they had to live on was what the girl could take from the men's pockets while they were sleeping. When she saw what Hansa had to trade—a brilliant white tear the size of an acorn, chased with all the colors of sunset and sea—she snatched it up.

"That's my fortune made," she said, and in exchange gave Hansa a compass, a waterskin, and boots to trade for her flimsy shoes.

"May the boots never waterlog," the merchant girl said. "May the waterskin never empty. And may the compass never lead you astray."

Now Hansa set out to find a ship with a maiden's name. She saw the *Luckjoy*. The *Greengage*. The *Ondine* and the *Azarias*. When she spied the *Lady Catherine*, she approached. Its captain was a woman with a shaved head, a crew of tattooed sailors, and a narrow look for Hansa when she traded the second of her Moon's tears for passage.

"It's worth my entire ship," she said, and took it.

The tear bought Hansa a bed belowdecks and the right to sit in the rigging. She loved her life at sea. The crew's sun-lined faces reminded her of her father's, and the briny air of the scent of his coat, and the movement of the ship of dreams she'd had, in the airless rooms of her grandmother's cottage. Every night she crept from bed to lie beneath the open sky, and the dancing forms of all her mother's sisters, and speak to the Moon.

Hello, grandmother.

The Moon told Hansa of the Winds and the Tides and the arrogant Sun, who spent his nights in a fiery country unreachable by land or sea. She told her of the rare white flowers that grew on her own hills and valleys, and of all their magical properties. Hansa wanted to pick those flowers. She wanted to wade in the Moon's wide rivers, and set sail to every unmapped island.

So you will, said the Moon. *My granddaughter was not made to have dirt beneath her feet.*

But even the Moon's protection was limited. She was sleeping the afternoon a storm came out of a cloudless sky. Beneath the Sun's hot eye the water rose, the sea whipping itself into waves that spun the ship like a toy.

The captain shouted into the squall, sending her sailors scattering over the deck. Hansa found herself trapped in the crow's nest as the ship tilted low, so perilously close to the water she knew it must touch, and all of them drown. She held on tight and looked into the frothing sea. Out of the murderous chop rose a face with a boiling white brow, eyes like whelks, and a mouth as wide as a whale's.

"Star's daughter," the face boomed. "I am the Tide who keeps watch over the waters when the Moon is young. What foolish errand has sent you to die at sea?"

"Are you my mother's husband?" she shouted, her words nearly lost beneath the water's crashing.

"I am his youngest brother," the Tide replied, each word a ship's-horn blast.

"Then you're very nearly my uncle," she said, squinting against the spray. "Will you help me, out of family feeling? I seek my mother at the rim of the world."

The Tide paused before giving a laugh that spun the ship a full turn, nearly flinging Hansa from her perch.

"I have no heart in which family feeling might reside. Nonetheless, I'll give you some advice. My brother keeps his secrets, and I don't know how to reach the world's edge. But our other brother might. He keeps sea wolves to serve him, and they swim farther and faster than any other creature. Seek him out. If he doesn't kill you, he just might help you."

His black-and-white face fell apart into foam, and the sea settled like a cat beneath a hand. Soon it was smooth as watered silk.

Hansa descended the mast into a crowd of hard-lipped sailors. They hadn't seen the Tide's face or heard their conversation. What they'd witnessed was a girl holding tight to the mast in an impossible storm, leaning over the sea to preach calmness until it listened.

They should've been grateful, perhaps. But Hansa was a captain's daughter and knew they wouldn't be. No one is more superstitious than a sailor at sea. She was very nearly unsurprised when, late that night, four rough hands dragged her from her bunk and up to the deck.

"Grandmother!" she cried, but the sailors were too quick. Hansa slept in her boots and was still trying to kick them off when she was thrown over the side of the ship. *Compass,* she thought as she fell, naming the things she had on her person. *Boots. Waterskin.*

The Moon's last tear.

She slipped it into her mouth for safekeeping just as she hit the surface of the sea. The water was mercury bright with moonlight above and all sharp teeth below, and the shock of it made her swallow the tear.

Grandmother! she screamed in her mind, fighting her way to the surface.

Patience, granddaughter, said the Moon. *This is all part of the tale.* Her light fell on the sea, and on the ship that was already too far to swim to, and on the four water-black heads that bobbed up around Hansa.

Mermaids. Their skin was gray, their hair painted colorless against the night. The nearest sliced Hansa's leg with a twitch of her serrated tail.

"Pretty little Star-child," she said, her voice syrup and salt and a seagull's scream.

"Not so pretty," the second one sniffed, moonlight catching on the points of her teeth.

The third dipped below the water to run a rough tongue over the fresh cut on Hansa's calf.

"And only half-Star," she said when she resurfaced. "You should have chosen land or sky. The sea doesn't want you."

"No last words, little mongrel?" said the fourth mermaid, mockingly. "You'll have less to say soon enough.

Now!" she cried out, and dove. The rest dove with her, each tugging Hansa by a hand or a foot.

But the girl had stayed quiet for a reason. The tear she'd swallowed had melted on her tongue like jellied blood, tasting of sea wind and oysters and ice. It slid down her throat, rooting in her belly and sending out shoots: into her arms, the skin there shading to gray. Into her legs, fusing them together, frosting them over with scales. Her eyes grew a shining skin to keep the water out and her rib cage broadened, hardened, becoming a treasure chest even the sea couldn't crack.

When she breathed in, she breathed the sea. Her throat and lungs were gilded into little waterways, so she could live on both air and ocean as the mermaids did.

"She's played a trick on us," one of them said sourly.

Another whipped Hansa's new tail with her own. "If she won't play fairly, neither will we," she said, and the four of them spun away. Hansa lost them quickly in the water.

There was nothing for it but to swim. Past fish with animal faces and down into a forest of sea fronds curved and carved like wooden screens. Her lashing tail carried her through cold that would scour the flesh off a sailor's bones, but Hansa was no sailor. All night she wound through the grasping sea forest, on and on, until the sun rose and turned the water pale. By its light she found a clearing where a roofless coral palace grew up from the sand. She swam through its mosaicked halls to a receiving room, where sat a throne made of the masts of drowned ships, lashed together with sea wrack. On it drifted a man the size of a giant, with black skin and sea-green hair. He watched her approach with interested eyes.

"Stars don't live long beneath the water, and humans even more briefly," he said. "Yet you're alive. How interesting."

Hansa could feel how the sea responded to his voice, how even her fishtail drifted in time to it. "Who are you?" she asked.

"I am the Tide who keeps watch over the sea when the Moon reaches her middle age. And you are the Moon's granddaughter. What would you have of me?"

"My mother's freedom. Your brother holds her captive at the rim of the world."

"I make it a point never to step between husbands and their wives. However." He leaned in, and the sea did, too. "My older brother has grown altogether too powerful. So long as he holds the Moon's daughter, he holds the Moon in his thrall as well. I will help you travel to the rim of the world, and I will tell you how to release your mother from her marriage bond."

He whistled and a hound came forward, or what must pass for one beneath the waves: a rippling thing of silver scales, holding in its mouth a sea-glass dagger.

"There is one way to break their bond: you must remove your mother's hand, the one that bears his wedding ring. This dagger will cut through any manner of bone, even that of Starfolk. Will you take it?"

Hansa nodded, but still the creature did not give her the dagger.

"It's a long way yet to the rim of the world," the Tide told her. "My wolves will only take you to the beginning of the end, for going any farther does strange things to travelers. They say you lose pieces of yourself, that far from the world's heart. Be wary, Hansa the traveler."

The wolf dropped the dagger into her hand and took her by the neck. It was joined by two of its sisters, and the three bore her up, out of the palace, into the great expanse of water overhead.

Hansa's skin began to burn. The arms of the sea were tightening, threatening to break her in their grip. As the tear's protection faded, the water was no longer alive to her. She took in a mouthful of salt just as the wolves broke the surface of the water.

They pulled her through the warm skim at the sea's very top, and let her sleep on their backs when she tired. They dove down to catch little creatures for her, briny things that slept in seashells and crackled between her teeth. Though she drank often from her waterskin, it never emptied. Mermaids paced alongside them for miles, calling out in their curdled voices, but did not dare come close. At night the stars broke from their dancing to blow Hansa kisses, and by day she watched the Sun and was curious. *Great-uncle,* she said to him in her mind. *Will you speak to me?* But the Sun is haughty, and rarely recognizes even his own children.

On the third morning Hansa felt her boots dragging over the rising seabed, before coming to rest in the shallows. The Tide's hounds had carried her over a journey's worth of sea, and must leave her now at the beginning of the end. They nosed around her hips, crafty eyes shining, and sped in three silver dashes back toward the deep.

She watched them go. Behind her lay the entirety of the sea and sky: here the fickle Sun, pulling clouds nearer to him, then burning them away. There the Moon, forever showing different versions of her face, and all her daughters dancing their ancient dances around her, with an empty space among them from which Hansa's mother had been torn. Behind her was day and night and sea and land and all the pages of her own history, before she became a traveler.

She turned her back on it and faced the rim of the world.

At the world's edge is one last wood. It's a foggy, tricksy place, where fine white mist turns the air to tulle. Hansa took her compass from her pocket and let it lead her through the wood.

It was full of more than mist, she learned. The Tide's second brother had warned it might take pieces of her away, but first it returned to her things she had lost. She followed the sound of her human grandmother's voice, and the landlocked scents of hot heather and bread and fire. There came the strains of a song she'd never heard, but knew. Her mother had sung it to her, in the handful of days they'd had together after Hansa was born.

The mist meant to beguile her, but her compass led her through. At last she reached the end of the last wood, and stepped onto the rim of the world.

The journey did take pieces of her away, but it was only after leaving the mist that she knew what those pieces were: they were her years, stolen away as she wandered. She walked into the woods a child and walked out an old woman, bones aching and vision dimmed. She held off grieving by telling herself this was one more enchantment she could undo.

At the world's end was a little house, two figures standing before it. The woman had blue eyes like Hansa's and the man gray hair to his hips. They did not touch each other, or speak, but there was peace between them. Hansa had gained age without much wisdom, and still she could see it.

"Who are you, who has traveled so far to see us?" the man asked pleasantly.

The woman said nothing. On the third finger of her smooth left hand, a ring of blue water spun.

"I've traveled far," said Hansa, in her cracked old woman's voice, "to release my mother from her marriage bond."

She knelt in front of the Star, who looked at her hazily.

"Mother," she said. "Do you know me?"

Then she took the Tide's dagger and sliced off her mother's left hand. The hand turned at once into starlight, dissipating in the air, and the ring shivered into droplets that pattered to the earth. The Star said nothing and looked at no one. In a liquid silver rush she leapt back into the sky.

The Tide watched her go with a look of great calm. "I'll win her again," he said. "Stars have hardly any memory at all. Did no one think to tell you that?" With a tilt of his hand, the droplets of his ring drew themselves together and swelled into a wide blue wave. It picked him up and carried him over the top of the misty woods, toward open sea.

Hansa stood alone on the sand, her skin weathered and her bones curved by the years she hadn't lived, that she'd lost in the mist of the woods.

I'm sorry, said the Moon.

She said it from very far away, but Hansa heard her all the same.

I cannot return your years to you, the Moon told her. *But I can offer you a kind of eternity.*

What kind? Hansa might have asked. And *How?* but she wasn't given the chance. Before she could speak or think, the Moon took her fragile body and flung it up among the stars.

Hansa was an old woman with her feet on the ground, then a different thing rising through the sky. Her skin peeled back, her bones boiled white, her thoughts came apart like the beads of a broken necklace. All the pieces of her that were left separated into new stars, picking out the shape of a girl. And so Hansa the traveler was granted her eternity.

On moonless nights, the stars that were Hansa let go their grip on the sky. They fall into the sea and shine beneath it, harrying the Tides. They rise like foam and come together into the body of a blue-eyed girl. She dives past the silver, through the blue, into the black. She runs her fingers through the seaweeds there, and remembers when her life was sunshine and captivity. She wonders which prison is preferred, a sealed cottage or the silence of the sky.

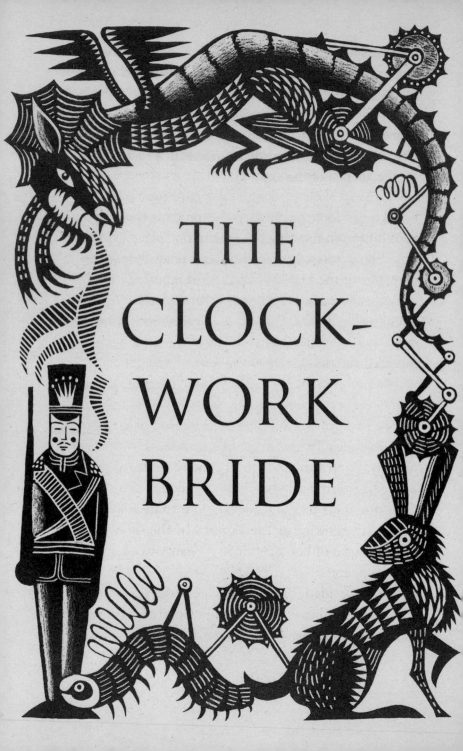

THE CLOCK-WORK BRIDE

The toymaker arrived in town on the back of rumors so vicious they cut the tongue. Fanciful, unsavory tales: that his hands could make anything, from clockwork assassins to skeleton keys. That baroque misfortunes befell those foolish enough to become his enemies, and kept him from roosting too long in one place. Most impossibly, it was whispered he had recently courted a daughter of the king. When the girl rebuffed him, he'd answered her rejection with a gift: a clockwork so enchanting she followed it out of her room one night and down to the hushed black ribbon of the river, where she followed the thing into its waters and was gone.

But the shop the toymaker opened overnight, packed to its corners with living dreams, was too beautiful to be the work of wicked hands. Though it was odd, the townspeople admitted, that no one could claim to have met the man himself. Behind his counter stood an aproned girl in a tidy braid, who smiled at the children and took their parents' coins. More than a few found themselves slowing as they walked by the shop, hoping for a glimpse of her face. Such a beauty wouldn't work for a monster.

It was decided, then. They were lucky the toymaker had come. And over time the dark cloud of rumors that nipped at his heels was forgotten.

Only Eleanor did not forget. Thirteen years old, she should've been past the point of longing for toys. Yet often she wondered what manner of toy was bewitching enough to coax a princess from her bed. A wee prancing stallion, perhaps, with a foaming mane, and flat metal teeth to pull the girl into the water.

Eleanor would risk anything to receive such a gift. She would follow it anywhere.

In a threadbare cloak and a dress she'd long ago out-grown, she walked between her mother and her brother, Thomas, through the kind of winter day that dulled its teeth on your bones. Everything she laid her eye on was damp or dim or scorched with cold—all but the toymaker's shop. Her mother's gaunt hand tightened on hers as they passed it, a silent warning not to stop. But a crowd of children stood out front, and that could mean only one thing.

"New toys today!" a boy called out, running past them. Eleanor tugged free of her mother and ran over the icy cobblestones, pushing her way toward the shop's bright window.

Inside she saw cut-paper ballerinas that spun on strings. Whole towns carved from wood and populated by tiny porcelain people. There were feathered masks and tin swords and dolls with clever eyes that blinked. But best by far were the clockworks. Animals and fair-ies and carriages and ships, butterflies that lifted the delicate glasswork of their doubled wings. Today the toymaker had added to his menagerie a poppy-red dragon, a pair of tussling fox kits, and a marvelous hare, which hopped and twitched its mottled ears just as if it were alive.

Eleanor could almost feel the greasy give of its brindle fur beneath her fingers, and smell its oiled-metal musk. As Thomas shoved in beside her, the scent of his hair—sweat and smoke and liniment—pulled her roughly from her daydreams.

"Why bother looking if you cannot buy?" one of the children said nastily.

Thomas dropped his head, but Eleanor favored the speaker with a knife-point smile. "Say one thing more," she said. "I beg you."

"I only mean to warn you," the girl replied, her voice a smooth blue river with rocks beneath it. "The toymaker punishes thieves. He'll drown you. He'll come for you in the night with his silver calipers."

I wish he would, Eleanor thought fiercely, her neck burning with shame and her fingertips pressed to the glass, their warmth turning its frost to wet jewels. *I wish, I wish, I wish.*

"Did you see the tin soldiers?" Thomas whispered from the pillow beside hers.

Eleanor shook her head.

"Or the forest made of glass? The kites? You only looked at the dolls, didn't you?"

She shook her head again. She didn't want to speak about the clockworks. Their clever brass pieces and neat metal chests, the places you could see their machinery and the places you couldn't, so they seemed like magic. The way their ticking perfection made her mouth dry up and her stomach twist around the part of her that always felt hungry.

Thomas squeezed her wrist. "Do you hear that?"

Eleanor shook her head a third time. She was tired of listening to her mother weeping behind the curtain that shielded her bed.

"Not that," he said. *"That."*

She listened, and the sound repeated itself. A sound too small to be heard, surely, but she heard it all the same. It was a *clump* and a *thump,* like a boot breaking through the crust that hardens over snow. She crawled from their bed to peer out the window, and wondered if she was already dreaming.

On the street below crouched the wonderful hare, the one she'd seen through the toy shop window. It had grown as big as a draft horse, and on its back sat a life-size tin soldier. Through the glass Eleanor saw his beckoning hand, the moonlight catching on the blond metal of his mustache.

She sprang back, already reaching for her cloak.

"What are you doing?" Thomas said.

She paused in the act of pulling on a boot. "What are *you* doing? Get your coat!"

"It's a trick," he said. "It must be."

All the sudden, delicate joy in her turned like old milk. "Stay behind then," she hissed, "and just see if I'll share with you."

Her brother lingered a moment, looking wounded, then gave in as he always did, pulling on his shoes and following her down the stairs.

Outside all was quiet, but for the mechanical breathing of the hare. Up close it was enormous, its sides giving off a steady machine heat. The soldier on its back, trim in a white uniform with blue piping, held tight to the velvet sails of the creature's ears.

"Come quickly," he said, in a high, sweet voice. "You've been invited by the toymaker to play!"

He lifted them onto the hare's back, his flexing fingers hard over Eleanor's waist. No sooner were they seated than they were off, bounding over the snow in great leaps. Eleanor felt the hard ticking of the hare's heart as her body in nightclothes slid over its fur. Beside her Thomas was taut as greenwood, his breath a cold white scuffle. When they reached the toymaker's shop the hare ducked its head, sending the children tumbling onto the frostbitten cobblestones.

The shop nestled among darkened buildings like a lit birthday cake. From its open door poured tinkling music-box notes and thick golden light. Gripping her brother's hand, Eleanor walked over its threshold.

There before them were all the toymaker's treasures. The paper ballerinas had grown to the size of children, with the small heads and slim limbs of women. They pirouetted in skirts of taffeta netting, their laughter scattering like light. The hare shrank down to size and rejoined the menagerie, which danced on hind legs and bumped friendly noses against the children's knees. The apple-cheeked woman who worked for the toymaker held out plump arms, moving from behind the counter to greet them. Eleanor laughed at the sight, triumphant at uncovering one of the shop's secrets: the woman was a clockwork, her lower half a solid wedge of unworked metal.

Shyly Thomas approached the soldiers, and soon he was leading a company of them in battle against the red dragon, whose muzzle licked with real flames. Pixies made of lantern light scurried over the walls, and the little ballerinas pulled Eleanor to her knees, touching her eyelids with glitter and her lips with paint, and nestling a paste-and-tin crown into her hair. When she rose again the tin soldier waited for her. His arms held and spun her so lightly she might have been a soap bubble. The laugh that broke from her lips seemed stolen from a different girl.

The hours wore on and Eleanor thought nothing of the hard, poor world beyond the toy shop's doors. The night was almost through when she remembered to ask after the toymaker, sensing dimly that she must thank him. She hoped he might send her home with an armful of gifts.

"The maker does not show his face," the animals sang, surging around her in a giddy whirl.

"Look for him behind his children,
We're his offspring, every one
Look for him behind the daydream
See his face before we're done!"

A host of rats swirled beneath the hem of Eleanor's nightgown. She shrieked at the tickle of their tails and the chatter of their little metal teeth. As the song's last note faded, the soldier dropped his hands from her waist. In two blinks he was toy-size and marching over the floor. The rats ran in a wet black line into an open toy box, followed by the soldiers. The ballerinas leapt skyward and caught hold of their strings, shrinking into flat paper figures with their arms outthrown. Soon the whole shop was tucked away and still. Early light tapped at the windows, and all that was left of the night was the crown in Eleanor's hair.

Her brother was nowhere to be seen.

"Thomas?" she whispered. Then she said it louder. Soon she was circling the shop, crying his name, fear tightening its grip on her throat.

"Have you lost him?"

Eleanor spun toward the back of the shop. The voice had come from behind a painted screen, made to look like a theater stage with its curtains tied back. Through its fabric she could see the figure of a man, too long and thin as a finger bone. He spoke again.

"Little girl who thought she had nothing, have you lost your brother, too?"

"What have you done with him?" She would not allow her voice to tremble.

"What have I done? I've given him the gift of all his dreams come true." The figure bowed, his spidery outline folding nearly in two. Then he stepped from behind the curtain.

He was a man unnaturally tall and extraordinarily dirty, his skin as oil-stained as his suit. Under the filth he was handsome, in a curdled, wicked way: eyes keen, bones sharp, mouth as wide and fleshy as a rotten fruit.

"Where is Thomas? Give him back."

"As you wish." The toymaker kneeled, heaving open a chest to reveal her brother curled inside it, fast asleep. Eleanor rushed to him, shaking his shoulder and calling his name, but he slept on.

"What have you done?" she cried. "Wake him up!"

The toymaker watched the slumbering boy, his face tender. "Would you interrupt his dreaming? And then how would my pretty things run? I can only do so much with ribbons and ratchet wheels. My creations feed on the dreams of children who lie asleep, spinning the enchantments I pluck from their heads. How many things might I make from this sleeper? And what would you give me to wake him instead?"

Eleanor reached for her brother, then stopped. He looked so peaceful. Here she stood, shivering in her nightgown, as he lost himself in visions that carried him far beyond the reach of long nights and bare cupboards and their mother's endless crying.

Envy wrapped cold green hands around her heart. Thomas had always been the easy child. Easy to love, at ease in the world. A comfort to her mother in ways she would never be. He could soothe her sorrows when Eleanor could not.

"Myself," she said. "I would give myself."

The toymaker twitched one hand, dismissively. "I have no use for hungry girls. I make beautiful things, curious things. What would I make of dreams with claws and teeth?"

Eleanor flushed. "I have nothing else to offer."

"Aha." He put up a finger. "You have nothing else *yet*. But one day you'll be a bride. On another you'll become a mother. And when your first child comes of age, it will be mine. Do you agree to my terms?"

Eleanor considered the life he laid out for her. A girl, then a wife, then a mother. A life in which the only mysteries open to her lay beyond the place where Death waited, tapping his pocket watch.

"I will have no children," she said. She'd seen her own mother in childbed twice. One baby was buried before it was old enough to speak, the other given to its father to live a kinder life somewhere else. Eleanor would never, ever become a mother.

"Have children or not, my terms are unchanged. Do you accept them?"

"I do."

Gently the toymaker touched Thomas's cheek, leaving a smudge of oil behind. The boy opened his eyes at once. It took longer for the dreamer's smile to leave his lips.

Sister and brother walked over the diamond-hard streets in their nightclothes and cloaks and boots. They let themselves into their quiet apartment, the whole place gone gray with their mother's sleeping breath. Eleanor lifted the toy crown from her hair and hid it away, then lay beside Thomas. He reached for her hand.

"Eleanor," he whispered. "I was having the most wonderful dream."

Thomas died at the end of winter. Since their night at the toymaker's he'd been dozy and drifting, and slipped so easily into fever he was gone before anyone knew he was ill. The sickness that took him swept through town and stole away more than half its children. By spring the toy shop had closed its doors and the toymaker moved away. No one could bear to see the playthings glinting through his windows with so many little ones lost.

Eleanor grew up. The night she spent playing in a wakeful toy shop faded to memory, then dimmed to a dream. She didn't think about the toymaker and her promise. Two summers after Thomas's death their mother, not so old and still beautiful, married a widower twice her age, and they moved into his house. Two more years came and went, and the old man took an increasing interest in giving his stepdaughter away. Soon there were dances held in his hall, one a week until Eleanor determined it would, in fact, be better to accept a young man's suit than to spend her life in clumsy courtship.

The boy she said yes to had a richer father and a softer heart than she deserved, and a romantic streak that allowed him to love her on the basis of her dark eyes and the moods he interpreted as shyness. Even Eleanor knew she was lucky.

On her wedding day her mother dressed her in a burden of white lace and combed her hair, looking into the glass over her daughter's shoulder. Though they were safe now, her mother's face still held the shadows of the hard years. "I have a gift for you," she said, her mouth almost smiling.

The thing she lifted into the light was made of tin cut delicately as lace, studded with paste diamonds. She settled it into her daughter's hair.

"I found it among our old things," she said. "Who knows where it came from. It's just a plaything, but isn't it pretty? It's good luck to wear a piece of the past on your wedding day."

The crown's fine teeth dug into Eleanor's scalp as she gripped her intended's hands and listened to the judge who married them. Its false stones threw little lights against the walls of his chambers. When she closed her eyes she saw a yellow-haired soldier and the warm speckled back of a clockwork hare.

Her new husband winced, then winked at her. *Don't be nervous,* he mouthed, turning his hand to show her where her nails had bitten into his skin.

There was always going to be a baby. Eleanor didn't accept that until she was too far gone to deny it, knuckles between her teeth to hold back the hysteria that threatened to leak from her throat. Her husband's face went so soft when she told him. There was nothing he wouldn't forgive her now: her impatience, her forgetfulness, her formless anxiety.

"All you must do," he said soothingly, "is take care of yourself and our child. Do nothing that might harm it, or you."

She tried not to laugh when he said that. She tried not to scream. In her dreams she was a child still, not yet pregnant, and Thomas lay in a toy chest. His fingers curving over its rim were bone white, were *bones*; he was trying to escape but he was too weak to rise. When he managed to pull himself out, he turned to show Eleanor the key in his back.

It would've been so easy, he said in his ticking, whirring new voice. *You could have saved me just by winding my key.*

She woke soaked in sweat. Soaked in more than sweat; her water had broken. For three breaths she thought she could outrun it. On the back of a brindle hare, the thighs of a soldier pressing on either side of her.

The first contraction swept the visions away, and her husband woke at the sound of her cries.

The baby was born with a coat of fine hair and a voice like a cat's. You could hide it in a seashell, that voice, to keep her safe. It was the kind of thing a witch might do. Eleanor drifted on waves of dreaming and the herbs the midwife gave her.

"The hair will fall out, in time," the midwife told her briskly, already at the door. "She was born too soon."

Eleanor slept to avoid looking at the child. While she slept, her husband filled her room with roses. It was late autumn and the flowers were scorched and frozen in turn, by the overfed fire and the chill bleeding through the windows. One by one they died, heads dropping, petals blackening, stems fuzzing over with scum.

All but one. One bloom remained: a perfect full-blown rose. Eleanor lifted herself from bed, breasts heavy with milk, and hobbled toward it.

It was cold against her fingertips. When she put an ear close, she could hear its meticulous tick. It was a clockwork rose.

They named the baby Arden, and she grew. It was natural that her mother's love should grow with her, but sometimes it seemed to Arden's father that his wife would prefer the girl be kept under glass. He indulged her protectiveness, was even relieved by it. She'd suffered badly through the pregnancy, and he'd worried—though he told no one of it, not even himself—she might not love the child as she ought. Then the baby came and they both loved her fiercely, and all was well until the morning of her first birthday.

Arden's father was still in bed when Eleanor cried out from the nursery, the baby's voice rising alongside her own. He found her standing by the crib, something cupped in her hands. Arden stood with her arms reached out, shrieking for the thing with blank ferocity. On instinct he snatched it from his wife and gave it to his daughter; at once she quieted and sat down to inspect the object, turning it over in her soft fingers. He had just time enough to see that it was a little clockwork caterpillar, prettily done, before his wife's slap cracked against his cheek.

Eleanor insisted the toy be destroyed. Her husband, steadfast for once in the face of her will, said she must give her reasons before he would do it. Because she would not, and because Arden screamed and wept and refused to eat when the thing was not near her, it was decided by nightfall that they would keep it.

Later he wished he'd listened to his wife, sensing in a vague way that the toy's arrival, and Arden's delighted obsession, marked the beginning of a change in both daughter and wife. Eleanor held Arden less often after that day, and weaned her without ceremony. Sometimes he caught her watching the baby and her toy with an expression both vivid and unreadable.

On the eve of Arden's second birthday, her caterpillar shed its carapace, clicked into the shape of an orange butterfly, and flew through an open window. Stunned by its transformation, the husband looked to his wife. She was watching the sky where the thing had disappeared with a look on her face that made his stomach seize tight.

Arden took its loss calmly. The next morning, on her birthday, they heard her laughing through the walls. When Eleanor would not rise, he walked to her bedroom alone. There he found the child sitting up, clapping at a clockwork kitten pouncing and tumbling over her rumpled bed.

The gifts came on every birthday. Eleanor did not like them, refused even to look at them, but never again suggested they be destroyed. She had more children: another girl, a boy. A fourth child who slipped away before it could be born. Among the three who lived, only Arden received gifts no one could explain. And only Arden was treated by her mother with a cool civility, an unmistakable distance that inspired her siblings to likewise view her more as visitor than sister. Her father tried to make up for it by loving her best, but being held at arm's length seemed to suit his firstborn child. She was forever sneaking off to be alone with her toys, always smiling over some memory or joke no one shared. As she grew up she became beautiful, but it was an impenetrable kind of prettiness. Nothing about her invited you to step closer.

As the years passed the gifts were increasingly a source of discord. In the days before her birthday Arden grew restless, snappish. In the days after she was secretive and silent, only to break, when she thought no one was near, into antic play. At eight she received a magnificent palace that opened on a hinge and was filled to the brim with tiny, intricate dramas: a prince and a chambermaid kissed, a crone bent over a spinning wheel, an adviser whispered into the ear of a king. Her father didn't like the knowing looks on the figures' faces, or the jealousy the gift prompted among his other children.

When she turned twelve Arden's gift was a baby doll. Over the space of a week the family realized the thing was aging, becoming more of a child each day. Arden rarely parted from it, tending to it as it aged over the course of one year, from baby to child to girl her own age, who could flutter its lashes and dance a minuet but neither slept nor ate nor spoke any word but *Arden,* and sat motionless in a chair when the girl was sleeping. The doll kept growing, to the age of a mother, then a grandmother, then a crone. The day before her thirteenth birthday, Arden couldn't stop weeping. The crone watched her for hours through filmy glass eyes, until, at midnight, its clockwork heart gave out.

The night before Arden's sixteenth birthday, her father couldn't sleep. His wife, too, was awake beside him, but he left her to her thoughts. They were no less opaque to him now than they'd been the day they married. He couldn't regret his choice of partner, but he wondered sometimes if their dreams looked anything alike.

It was late. So late it was early. Their first child would be sixteen tomorrow. *Of age,* he thought dimly. Tomorrow, the girl would come of age. Hours passed and neither parent shifted from their sleeplessness. The sun came up, its light threading the eye like a needle. It outlined Arden as she let herself into their room.

"Look," she said. Sixteen but still a child in her nightgown, her voice turned up at the oddity of what lay in her hands. She would never have come to them if it hadn't unsettled her. "I got my gift."

It was a clockwork hare with brindle fur and a gaze of black glass. On its back, trim in blue and white, was a little tin soldier.

————

Arden was unhappy with her gift. Though the soldier was handsome, she supposed, and the hare hopped obligingly about the room, its velveted nose quivering, the gift was childish. The thing she liked best about it was the way her mother seemed to think it might bite her, as if it were an ogre or an enchanter, not a silly tin man on a strange little mount. Arden sent it hopping into the parlor where her parents were reading just to hear her mother's gasp. If she could not be loved by her mother, she could at least distress her.

Eleanor had always hated Arden's gifts, had always ruined her birthdays with mute protest of the glinting mysteries her daughter had grown up expecting to receive. Sometimes Arden felt there was a little piece of clockwork inside her, too, that ticked down to each birthday. When she woke and saw her newest gift beside her, the sight wound her up like a key, made her happy again, and lively, taking away the loathsome lethargy that grew over her like ivy. The gifts were her best friends, the unseen hand behind them her greatest benefactor. When she was young she imagined the giver to be some faraway queen, her real mother. As she grew older she decided the gifts came from a prince. Arden showed her true self only in the presence of these toys, speaking to them of her wishes and wonderings. And when she lay down at night they followed her beyond the borders of sleep, filling her dreams with the rhythmic tick she liked better than any sound in the world.

Usually on the night of her birthday Arden slept with her new gift beside her, so she could wake in the morning and see it first thing. But this year the hare and soldier were dropped on the floor, away from her. She slept fitfully. The sound that woke her was the muffled falling of early snow. It made a particular kind of quiet, dense as cake.

There was a man in her room. She held herself still as she realized it, her breath sawing against the silence. He was smart in his uniform, handsome in his blond mustache. Behind him, the hare had become massive. Its eyes collected the light.

When the soldier kissed her she could feel the glossy smoothness of his skin, the scratch of his tin mustache. The kiss pierced and spread, filling her with a drowsy weight.

"Come quickly," he whispered. "You've been invited by the toymaker to play."

In the white-and-silver light of the season's first snow, filled with the soporific of her first kiss, Arden pushed back her bedclothes. She let the soldier pull her onto the hare's broad back.

Arden's fingers slipped over the hare's fur as it bounded through the streets, turning its head from time to time to peer at her through the glassy shell of one eye. They went fast through town and faster through the woods. Arden saw things from the hare's back that let her know the world was bigger than she'd imagined it to be. The soldier's hands on her waist were another kind of knowledge. She cried out once, when a hanging branch ran its finger over her cheek, but neither mount nor companion replied.

They came at last to a castle that ambled over its plot like a city's worth of houses drawn together. As they approached she could see more clearly its eccentricities. Its window boxes were full of sharp flowers, copper birds hopped and pecked on the sills. Women stood in the windows watching their approach, waving embroidered handkerchiefs.

At the threshold of the castle, the tin soldier left her. Arden paused only a moment before opening its doors, her eyes widening at what lay before her.

She was looking at the contents of her dreams. The older, childish ones. Rose-furred ponies with eagle's wings wheeled and spun about the rafters, calling to her in sweet voices. A party of white cats played games on the floor, dressed in a kingdom's worth of finery.

And everything she saw was a clockwork. The air hummed with a steady tick: the rhythm she longed to feel behind her own rib cage, where her living heart sped and slowed and tapped out its unpredictable beats.

She ran ahead. Up a winding stair, through more rooms full of things she'd dreamed. Here a flock of fairies with tinsel wings, zipping over a river of blue sugar water dotted with croaking toads. There, a ballroom where dancers spun beneath a painted ceiling. Slinky greyhounds threaded through her legs, and a metal mermaid sang to her from a bathtub lined with garnets.

The visions grew darker as she climbed. Arden recognized images from her nightmares, and from dreams so secret she would've shuddered, anywhere else, to see them held to the light. She walked through bedchambers and sitting rooms, halls and alcoves. She saw life-size tin dolls with the faces of her family, her mother holding tightly to the hand of a little boy she didn't recognize. As Arden walked through rooms filled up with her own longings, she felt those longings fall away. She did not wish to run to her mother, to call to her father. She felt neither fear nor shame, only a curiosity that drove her ever onward, to the place's very top.

There she found a grand receiving room, hung with tapestries and fit for a king. At the room's far end, past frozen rows of kneeling metal attendants, a man did sit on a throne. But he was not a king.

Arden walked slowly toward him, the air vivid with the ticking of a hundred handmade hearts. She took in the filth of his suit, too small to hold his spider's limbs, and the oil smeared over his sunken cheeks.

Here was a creature of flesh, the only one in the castle. She knew him for what he was: the giver of her birthday gifts. All the lovely stories she'd told herself about him curled in on themselves like burning paper and drifted away.

"Kneel," he told her. Arden's mind did not wish to, but her body obeyed. As she crouched before him a great stillness came over her, settling her racing heart. It slowed. It steadied. It *tick tick tick*ed.

"My child." His smile was tender. "Did you like your presents?"

Arden nodded, her chin dipping down then up. *Tick tick.*

"You are just as I imagined you would be," he said. "In all the years I've built this house of wonders, fed on your dreams."

"For me?" she asked him, though she already knew. "All for me?"

The toymaker's eyes roamed over her face. "All for you, all *of* you. You will be—you are—my bride. A girl raised on clockworks, to be mine."

Arden frowned. He did not notice.

"I thought myself capable of anything," he said, "yet I could not make myself a companion. Could not *build* myself a bride. No automaton's skin is as soft as a woman's, nor do the blushes in it rise and fall, nor does she speak so naturally nor eat and drink without her workings going up in sparks. Nor can she take my hand. Nor can she share my bed.

"But *you.* All your life, you have dreamed to the ticking of my creations. And what is a child but her dreams? My toys have slept beside you, traveled with you into sleep, made your spirit as surely as your flesh was made by your mother. Press your hands to your heart, and feel how you belong to me."

She did, and felt under her fingers a cool ticking.

"You will marry me," said the toymaker. "With all my lesser workings to witness."

Arden raised her head. "Will I?"

The man on the throne did not hear. "Now stand up, and take my hand."

His voice was unsteady; it shivered with desire for a prize long deferred. Any woman's heart would've quailed to hear it.

But Arden's was no longer a woman's heart. The thing that beat in her chest had hardened, steadied, become a thing of cogs.

Always she had prized her ability to hold herself apart from the world. Where her siblings clung, to their parents and each other, she stood alone. This maker of clocks could not take credit for all she had become.

"I am not yours to command," she said.

He smiled at her, indulgence edged with malice. "You know so little of the world and of men. Do not make the lessons I must teach you any harder than they ought to be."

Arden looked at the man on his throne, this man of meat with a heart like a mouse's heart. "I am my own," she said. "I belong to me." Her eyes caught the light and held it, and his pitiful heart became, at last, afraid.

Now she looked over the watching crowd of his creations. They were made to answer to the man on the throne, just as she was made to be a dutiful daughter, and reshaped to be an obedient wife. Even a made thing can change its nature.

"Stand up," she told them.

Stiffly they rose, the hot sweet scent of gears and oil overtaking the odor of the toymaker's fear.

"Do you wish," she asked them, "to belong to yourself?"

Their glass eyes glittered. A whispering assent rose up from their metal tongues.

"Then let us show our maker what it is to be free."

The toymaker's army advanced slowly at first, then faster as their limbs learned the trick of operating without his leave. Beneath their metal hands the toymaker did not come apart in gears and the shine of hot oil, but in torn flesh and spilled blood.

And Arden, the liberator of the clockwork court, was made their queen. Despite the wishes of the toymaker, she never became a bride.

Sometimes on the road you may hear her coming, in her carriage attended by clockwork men. You'll know her by the flash of her eyes and the ticking of her undiscoverable heart. If you linger too long on the path she may sweep you away to her castle of countless wonders, to serve as entertainment, for a time, to those who reside there. But it rarely goes well in her court for those of flesh and blood, so you'd best take care not to linger.

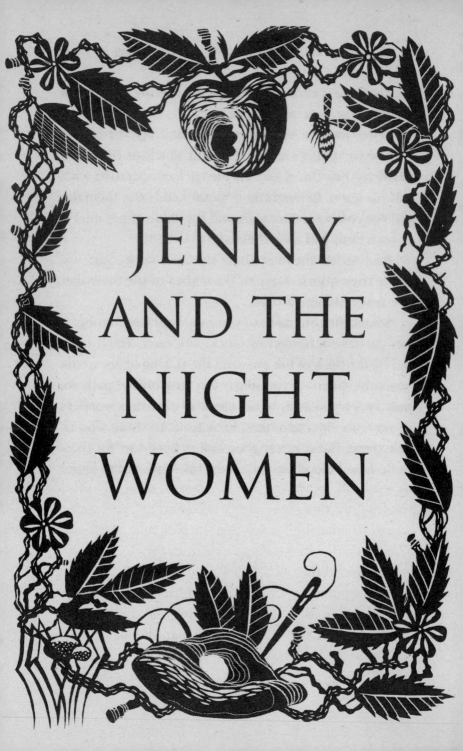

JENNY AND THE NIGHT WOMEN

A farmer and his wife, heartbroken because they could not bear a child, prayed for the gods to give them one, but there were no gods to hear. And so, because they knew the way of things in their part of the world, they got their child through different means.

In spring, the wife swallowed the pink-and-white petals of an apple blossom. So eager was she to do it, she didn't see the creep of brown at the flower's center—it had half rotted with rain.

By summer, the blossom had ripened and unfurled, turning to fruit in her belly.

In autumn, the woman felt sick to her soul.

In winter she retched and retched and vomited up an apple. It was red and crisp and delicious, its juice sweet as wine and its skin firm like the skin of a drum.

She ate the fruit with ferocious appetite, swallowing the core along with the flesh. At the fruit's heart was a circle of soft brown rot, but the woman didn't know it. She felt only joy as her belly swelled and ripened. In the course of time she bore a child, a pink and white and beautiful girl, with a core of hidden decay.

She named the girl Jenny. Because they'd waited for her so long and so longingly, the farmer and his wife spoiled the child. There was nothing she wanted that she didn't get. Day by day, year by year, she grew worse and worse. In her rose-painted room, among her many toys, she played alone, because no child ever played twice with Jenny.

The girl was ten when her father began to fear their doting might come with a price. "She's a grown girl and a farmer's daughter," he told his wife. "Not a princess. Who will marry her if she thinks she's royalty?"

Reluctantly, Jenny's mother agreed. The girl would inherit their farm one day, and would need a husband to help her work it. A woman alone on such ripe land was too sweet a lure. And though she wouldn't say it, she sensed a darkness in her apple-blossom girl. It was decided between them that they would no longer obey their daughter's every whim.

Soon after that, as she always did, Jenny asked for a kitten from the barn cat's litter. She kissed its nose and nuzzled its neck and dragged it about in a flour sack, laughing to hear its pitiful cries. The sack was stained with the kitten's fear when her mother yanked it away and set the creature free.

Weakly she scolded Jenny for her cruelty, but the girl only laughed. That night, her mother found the urine-soaked flour sack where Jenny had left it, laid atop her pillow.

The sight of it hardened her heart. Next time, she swore, she would not be so easy on the girl.

As the weeks went on, she taught herself to deny Jenny. No more milk in her bathwater and cake when she cried. No new shoes because she stamped off a heel in a fury, no new dolls because she cracked the limbs of the ones she no longer loved.

Jenny didn't scream over these new restrictions as her mother feared she would. She did not throw herself to the floor in a fever and weep. She looked at her mother with wide blue eyes, considering her in silence.

She was changing, the woman dared to believe. Her good girl, her apple child. Soon she would be as sweet as the fruit she sprang from.

Each morning Jenny's mother rose by dawn light weak as tea. She worked by her husband's side as the light thickened to honey then deepened to bathwater blue. In the evening, purified by sweat and the limpid air, she bathed her face and changed into a clean dress for dinner.

On one such evening she paused at the threshold of their farmhouse, ill at ease. The house seemed darker than it ought to be, the air tarred with iron and sugar. She stood a moment, breathing it in, as her dusk-dazzled eyes cleared.

She'd seen pieces of a shipwreck once, thrown up onto the shore of the Hinterland Sea. She thought of that now, taking in the wreckage of Jenny's revenge.

Everything in the room that could be smashed was in pieces. All the fine things she'd collected, the whittled figures and the pair of baby boots lovingly kept, a small painting of a mermaid and the blown-glass iris she'd carried on her wedding day. Flour and sugar were sifted over the floor like sand, gathering in dusty hillocks and sparkling drifts. Slicks of egg and their shells mixed with glass dust beneath her heels.

Jenny's door was locked, and when her father tired of

pounding his fists on it he smashed off the knob with a hatchet. The girl sat on her bed in a pink-and-white dress, her eyes like the empty cups of bluebells. All her belongings were spotless, untouched.

The sound of her mother slapping her cheek rang out like another thing breaking.

Never in her life had Jenny been struck. Holding her face, she ran from the house, over her parents' fertile fields, and into the woods. She fled like an animal, without purpose or plan. At first she was warmed by her fury. Then she grew frightened, as the forest's familiar edges gave way to something wild and unknown.

The stars were out when she spied a glimmer of light through the trees, which became the orange glow of a campfire. The sight made her mouth go dry with desire, for food and warmth and someone, perhaps, to lead her back home. Sitting on a fallen log beside the fire was a girl her own age, dark hair hanging in tangles to her waist. She spoke in a voice far older than her face.

"Go on your way or sit beside me, but make your choice."

Jenny came forward on tired feet, one hand tugging at her hair.

"Please," she said, tilting her head sweetly. "Won't you help me? I'm cold and hungry and lost in the woods."

"Foolish of you to lose yourself, wasn't it?"

Jenny straightened. "It wasn't my fault," she snapped.

And without prompting she told the stranger what her mother had done. The girl listened so intently, Jenny invented a few new sins to make the tale longer. By the end of it, she believed they were true.

The girl stirred the fire. "Your mother deserves to be taught a lesson. Your father, too, for allowing her to treat you this way."

There was an edge to her voice that Jenny recoiled from. There was rot in her, that was true, but she wasn't yet rotted through. She could sense what lay beneath the stranger's words: a dark mischief that promised a hard ending.

But the girl by the fire was clever. When she saw Jenny pull away, she changed tack. "Someone as pretty as you," she said, "should be treated like a princess."

Jenny leaned in.

"Yes," the girl said thoughtfully. "You must play a trick on your parents, to teach them. That they mustn't underestimate you, or learn to say no. Once they start saying it, they'll never stop. I will tell you, Jenny, what you must do."

Her next words took the shape of an incantation that buzzed inside Jenny's ear. "Take a needle," she said.

"Take a stone
and Prick their heels thrice.
Bloody the stone and bury it low
and let the Night Women come."

Jenny tugged absently at her ear. "Bury the stone?"

"Beneath their window," said the girl. "To invite the Night Women in."

"Who are the Night Women?"

The girl smiled, or perhaps she only showed her teeth. One of her incisors was dark with decay. Another overlapped it, as if to hide it from view. "They're as beautiful as you, though not so good. If you're brave enough to let them in, they'll give you just what you deserve."

Then she pointed Jenny toward a path she'd missed, a beaten dirt trail between trees. "Now go along home. The quicker you return, the quicker you can punish them."

Jenny left her sitting by the fire in her cape of tangled hair, smiling her brown-and-white smile. The walk back was quicker than she thought it would be. Soon she heard her own name, then found her parents wading through the trees, her mother weeping and her father holding a lantern. They fell on their daughter with tears of relief.

In their arms she forgot the girl in the woods. Frightened at having almost lost her, Jenny's parents were obedient again. Her father bought her a dozen dolls and a bouquet of red glass roses. Her mother came home with a pair of satin boots with fifteen buttons apiece and a bracelet of soft gold. They gave them to her like offerings, and for a time the girl was satisfied.

But wickedness was as much a part of her as blue eyes and a heedless heart. They could not deny that she was as she had always been, prone to fits of rash temper and cruel tricks. They indulged her for a while, but the day came when they did not.

And every time they scolded or denied her, Jenny remembered the girl in the woods. She forgot the old voice and the hard mischief, remembering instead the girl's praise and the warmth of her fire. The promise of the Night Women, who would give Jenny what she deserved.

And when she'd had her fill of being thwarted, Jenny did what the girl told her she must.

Jenny took a needle, and she took a stone. She waited until her parents were asleep and slipped into their room. Their faces were in darkness, so she did not have to see them as she pulled up the coverlet to reveal their feet. With her needle she pricked the hardest parts of their heels, where they wouldn't feel it. When she smeared their blood over the flat gray stone she'd found in the garden, the very last bit of her that wasn't yet spoiled gave a shudder.

As she dug up the earth outside her parents' window and buried the stone beneath it, that last unspoiled bit at her center blackened and curled. She was rotten clean through.

Jenny lay awake in the dark of her bedroom, waiting to see what might come. Wind rattled the windows, branches tapped on the glass.

Rattle, rattle. Tap, tap.

Scratch, scratch.

She sat up in bed.

The pitch of the rattle was rising, till it almost sounded like the chatter of voices. The tapping steadied, falling into a rhythm like the drumming of long fingernails. Then came the shatter-*thump* of breaking glass.

Jenny fell back, pulling up the covers till they hid all but her eyes. The voices were closer now, musical and sweet. Someone laughed. Then a moan, quick and cut off in the middle. Her mother's?

She strained to hear, motionless, not daring to breathe, and—

The voices died away, turned down, were nothing more than the rattling wind. The fingernails were only branches.

Jenny turned onto her side and fell asleep.

She woke with cold hands and a hollow head. Before the sun was fully up, her mother opened her bedroom door.

She was smiling. Her hair was braided back, and in her hands was a breakfast tray.

"For you, my love. All the things you like best."

Jenny's father waited behind her. There was a thin line of sweat above his lip, and his foot would not stop tapping.

The breakfast was everything Jenny wanted, all of it hot and sweet. Still she felt uneasy. As she swallowed her final bite, she understood why.

It was her mother. Usually she smelled of butter and sweat, of heat and hay. But when she leaned in to kiss Jenny, she hadn't smelled of any of those things. She'd had no scent at all.

Jenny's father bought her a horse. She'd always wanted her own, but he'd said she was too young. Now she sat proudly atop a piebald mare with a soft brown mane and a saddle of glistening leather. Her father put a hand to the horse's haunches and the animal startled, skin shuddering beneath his fingers like they were fleas.

Her parents watched as she learned to ride, their faces vivid with pride. Their eyes were on Jenny all the time now. They watched her ride, watched her eat, watched her play with the new toys they gave her, beautiful things of glass and metal and wood wrapped in rustling blue paper.

Jenny's horse was her favorite gift. The animal was gentle and patient, and loving her might've healed the rot at Jenny's core, in time. But a week after her father brought the horse home, after Jenny had swung into the saddle, he moved too close to the creature's head. The mare jerked away from him, baring her teeth.

The sun was behind him, so Jenny could not be sure. But it seemed to her that her father showed his teeth back, in a grin that made his head look smaller and his mouth seem terribly large. When he reached for the mare, she reared up, throwing Jenny into the dirt.

Jenny landed hard on her back. Through her pain she heard the horse hammering over the dirt and the chilling sound of her mother's scream. She ran to her daughter, but Jenny's father ran after the horse.

Jenny was on her knees when a second scream came from the fields, a beast's cry of fear and pain. When her father returned, his shirt was slick with the mare's blood.

Jenny wept, and her parents paced outside her door.

"Jenny, Jenny," they cried. "What can we do for you?

What can we give to you? Please, tell us, what will make you happy?"

When she finally opened the door, the sight of them was startling. Her father was red-eyed and narrow in his shirt, while her mother seemed to be swelling, her limbs and belly and mouth voluptuous. The way they beamed at her gave Jenny the stuffed-sick feeling of having eaten too much sugared cream.

"Leave me alone," she said unsteadily. "I will be happy if you leave me alone."

Their faces twisted, but they nodded and went away.

Her mother came back in the night. She sat by Jenny's bedside and stroked her hair, worrying all its knots free. Her scentless breath touched her daughter's cheek, and Jenny tried to make herself still. She lifted one eyelid, just enough to peek.

Her mother was smiling down at her, always smiling. It was a smile so wide and radiant her face could hardly hold it. It looked like someone had grabbed the sides of her mouth and tugged.

Jenny squeezed her eyes shut and tried to sleep.

Always at night now she heard the whispering, the fingernails on glass. Her days were an endless parade of gifts and grasping affection. When she came too close, her mother stroked her cheek. She kissed her forehead, held her hands, buried her nose in Jenny's hair. Jenny twisted away, but her mother's smile never wavered. Her husband grew thinner and she grew thick. Her body sweetened, it swelled like a tick.

"I am growing you the loveliest gift," she told Jenny one day. She rubbed her stomach, nails long and curling. "You'll be so pleased when I give it to you. Kiss my cheek now, and I will feed you chocolate. I will give you toys. You will have all the good things you deserve."

Her belly was round as an apple now. Perhaps a baby was dreaming inside it, in the place where Jenny once roosted. But where was her father? The days melted into each other like sticky candies, and it felt a long time since she'd seen him. If he'd gone to town, he'd be back by now, with an armful of dolls. His fields were empty, and his chair, and his side of her mother's bed. If he wasn't there, who was it her mother whispered with when Jenny heard whispering in the night?

The same ones, perhaps, whose fingernails tapped the glass.

One morning Jenny rose before breakfast and walked down the hall. Her mother's door was open just enough that she could see her dressing through the crack. Her feet were bare and the one Jenny had pricked looked like a dead thing, black and purple with bruises. A fizzing cloud of flies lifted and fell over something on the floor that Jenny could not see. The room's scent reminded her of the smell of the yard on butchering day.

Her mother looked up from tugging her boots on. She smiled and licked a dark smear from the corner of her mouth. With one hand she reached out to Jenny.

"My love," she said.

All that day Jenny let her mother kiss her cheeks and eyelids and chin. She ate the sugary foods that were fed to her, that melted on her tongue like sweet air. She allowed her mother to comb her yellow hair.

And when it was night, and her mother asleep at last, Jenny rose from her bed. By moonlight she packed dresses and handkerchiefs and all the coins she'd stolen over the years and hidden beneath her bed. Her dolls and stuffed kittens and glass roses she left behind.

She thought she'd sneak out by the window. But the rustling had already begun, the tap-tapping on the glass. She crept through the dark house instead, its empty rooms that smelled of sugar and dust and death.

Her mother waited by the door. Moonlight threw the swollen shadow of her belly across the floor.

"Were you going away, my Jenny?" Her voice was woeful, but her smile was bright. "Were you going to leave me? If I had lost you, I'd never be happy again."

Her tongue ran over her lip. Had it always been so long, so wet and red?

"But I didn't lose you, and I never will. You are my child. I want you close, my Jenny. As close as you can come."

"I don't want to," Jenny whispered.

Her mother's fingers on her belly tapped and tapped. "But you always want. Come closer now, so I can whisper of all the things I'm going to give you."

She inched forward on long bruised feet. She rubbed her belly and the thing that lay inside it, ready to become something new. Her smile was wide and wider, a grin, then a gash, then an unpeeling.

Jenny was sweeter than you'd think. It's always that

way with rotten things. When her mother was done, she lay down for the last time. Her body made a curious sound as it fell away from the thing her stomach carried, like a husk from a cherry.

The thing she'd birthed stretched. It untucked. It was shaped like a shadow that warped and ran and bent in odd places. With a quiver and a sigh, it gathered itself into the form of a woman. Beautiful, with fingernails made to scratch. Jenny's blood on the floor was red as candy, and her mother's gathered in black pools, reflecting moonlight like the glass eyes of a doll. The Night Woman was wet with it as she let herself out into the open air, to join her sisters.

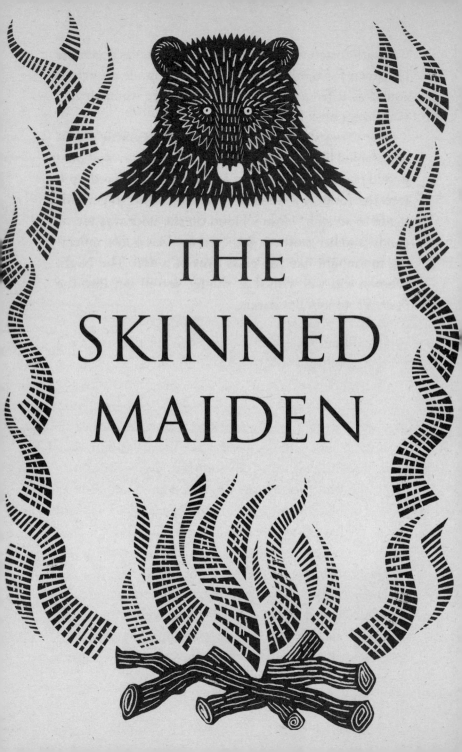

THE
SKINNED
MAIDEN

There are as many ways to take a wife as there are maids to marry.

Find a girl who catches your eye. Ply her father with coins, woo her mother with words. Make a woman yourself, out of petals or birdseed or snow. Blood for the lips, ash for the hair, be careful what you choose to make her heart. Wipe the filthy cheek of a drudge: under the dirt she might be beautiful, fit to be wed.

Now take a piece of her she can never get back, that she'd follow you to the rim of the world to retrieve. Bear your children, bake your bread, bide her time, all for a chance at staying close to that thing you've stolen away.

Her heart, perhaps. Or her skin.

An unwed prince is a dangerous thing. One such man was hunting in a summer wood when he came upon three bears standing upright beside a river, conversing. One had fur as white as the stones in a wedding ring. Another had fur as black as the ashes in a beggar's cup. The third was as golden as the center of a flame. The prince settled himself between two trunks and nocked an arrow to his bow, waiting to see what they might do.

"Shall we bathe ourselves, sisters?" said the white bear. They reached up and peeled the fur from their necks, from their faces and shoulders and limbs, revealing beneath their bearskins three maidens, one white-haired, one black-haired, and one with hair of gold. All three were beautiful, but it was the golden-haired maiden who pricked the prince's heart.

He watched as they bathed then stretched out bare in the sun. When its heat had dried them, they stepped back into their skins, nuzzled each other's cheeks, and wandered into the woods in three directions.

Each day the prince returned to the river to watch the beauties remove their bearskins and bathe. Each day his desire for the golden maiden grew, until he knew no other woman could please him. Stepping from the trees, he seized her shining fur.

The maidens looked up from the river, bodies bare and eyes flashing.

"I will take your bearskin," the prince told his yellow-haired girl, "unless you agree to marry me."

Swiftly she rose from the water, walking over the bank till she was a hand's breadth from the prince.

"I'll marry you," she said. "But first we must kiss to seal our agreement."

Enchanted by her nearness, he reached greedily for the girl. As he fitted his fingers to her waist, the bearskin fell from his grasp. Fish-quick she slipped inside it, becoming again a great beast, claws and teeth set to rend. The prince saw he had been bested, and retreated before he could be killed.

He went home in a red rage. He beat his horse, slapped the servants, overturned his wine. Watching his fit of temper from her usual seat was his father's mistress. She had lived in the castle since the queen's death, and was known for her gifts with magic. Long had this witch despised the prince for his cruelty and caprice, and longer had she dreamed of eliminating him, thus chiseling a path for her own illegitimate son to inherit the throne. The old king's recent illness had only made her more eager to dispose of the prince.

She approached him once his fury had cooled to a sulk.

"What is upsetting you, my boy?" she asked, hiding her hatred in soft words. He searched her face for signs of mockery and, perceiving none, told her of the three maidens in their bearskins and how he had been fooled. The witch made her face grave, even as her heart filled with dark joy.

"If you wish her to submit," she said, "you must burn her skin of yellow fur. Once you've done so, she will not be able to refuse you."

And the witch removed herself to her chambers, certain she was sending the young man to his death at the claws of the gold-furred bear. But the prince was cheered, eating and drinking heavily and falling that night into happy visions of pliant women. He woke refreshed and returned on horseback to the woods. He built a fire a little ways from the bears' clearing, then climbed into a tree to conceal himself. When the beasts arrived they looked behind each trunk, but did not spy him among the leaves.

Slowly, slowly, the prince crept to the ground. When the maidens were distracted by their bathing, he stole over the grass and seized up the golden bearskin. It was unwieldy in his arms, smelling of juniper and sweat. When he threw the skin on his fire, the golden maiden screamed as if it were her body that was burning. The fur went up quick as kindling, flaking to ashes before her cry had died away.

"Now," said the prince, returning to the riverbank, "I claim you as my bride."

The girl's eyes burned hotter and harder than his campfire. Already her sisters had stepped back into their skins.

"You will never see me again," she told him, "not a tooth nor a nail." And, climbing onto the back of the white-furred bear, she disappeared into the woods.

The prince went home even angrier than before. He tore at his shirt and kicked his dogs. He rushed to the witch's chambers, set on beating her for her bad advice. If she was surprised to see him alive, she did not show it. Before he could reach her she threw a fistful of fine green powder into his face, which filled his head with a sweet stupor. When he could think again, he was lying on her couch, his temper soothed.

The witch had calculated quickly while the young man was under her spell. She could not move against him without drawing the suspicion of the king, but chance had contrived to make for him a more danger-ous foe. If she could be clever, the problem of the prince might soon be solved. She knew that nothing fought so hard as a cornered creature; she must convince him to corner his maiden once more.

"This girl is more headstrong than we realized," she

said. "You are a lucky man: there's no prize sweeter than the prize hard-won. You've taken her skin of fur, it's true. But if you want her to truly be yours, you must take her woman's skin as well."

So determined was he to win his maiden, the prince did not question the advice of the witch. He saddled his horse and took to the roads alone. Knowing the bears would not return to the river, he traveled far and wide, disguised as a peddler, and sat at roadside inns each night with open ears. He heard many tales, of singing bones and frozen men and girls who became stars. And one weary night, he heard the tale he was listening for: of two bears and a wild maiden who ran together in the woods, and slept inside a circle of alder trees an hour's ride from the inn where he sat.

He set out at once. When he reached the alder clearing his heart quickened. There lay his own bright maiden, asleep between the white- and the black-furred beasts. Quickly he let two arrows fly into the necks of the bears. They woke just long enough to die, as the prince overpowered the maiden.

He held her face between his hands, her hair spilling like molten metal over his fingers. For a moment his heart shrank from the thought of what he must do. Then she turned her head and bit through the meat of his palm.

Pain turned his rind of pity into wrath. From his belt he pulled a knife. By the light of the moon, kneeling in the blood of her slain companions, he skinned the maiden.

She did not bleed. She did not scream. Her skin came away as easily as a fruit's peel. He rolled it up, tucked it into his pack, and considered the prize he'd won.

The maiden lay between his knees, beneath his blade, all of her pulsing and churning and unmuffled. Her curving bones, her throbbing heart, the parts of her he could not bear to look at. Even her thoughts could be seen, the violence in them leaving soft indents on the air. She did not run or weep or beg. She only looked at him.

"Give me back my skin," she said.

But she didn't move, neither to strike out at him nor to escape. The witch was right. His beloved had become defenseless, defeated. With eager hands, certain now of his victory, the prince made a fire and held her woman's skin over it, close then closer, until the air sizzled with rendering fat. "You'll obey me," he told her. Sweat made pale drops on his lip. "You'll be my loving bride."

Before he could thrust her skin entirely into the flames, she held out one delicate hand, all flexing tendon and salt-white bone. The prince took it.

They rode on horseback to his castle. He saw faces in the trees as they rode, of wolves and deer and other beasts who watched them with mournful eyes. The girl was bare in his arms, wet against his shirtfront. They reached the castle at sunset, the light pouring over his maiden like red honey. The witch saw them from her window, and gnashed her teeth to know her enemy still lived. Then she steadied herself and walked to the yard, ready to greet the prince and his stolen bride with false exclamations of joy.

But her tongue was stopped at the sight of the plundered girl. Heedless of the witch's horror, dazzled by his own triumph, the prince called out in a high humor.

"I have returned," he said, "and with me my happy bride. Bring a judge to my chambers, we wish to be wed."

The maiden watched the prince as the binding words were spoken. When the time came for her to accept him, she said again: "Give me back my skin."

He silenced her with a kiss.

The prince hid the skin. He hid it so well he almost forgot where he'd tucked it. For many weeks after their wedding he kept his new bride close at hand. She shared his hours, sat in council with him when he was required, attended him at every meal. He savored the fear her strange form struck in the hearts of lesser men. His father's men, who would one day answer to the prince, and to the wife who sat beside him.

She would be a good queen, obedient and beautiful and belonging utterly to him. Her new face was not the one he'd fallen in love with, but it was the one he had made for her. He had tamed a wild thing, and life together was a game they played. She slipped off to search for her skin—pacing the halls, sliding behind tapestries, digging to the backs of old wardrobes—and he followed after, bringing her always to heel.

Though it was true he could not touch her easily.

There was no place for his hands to find purchase. He had dresses made for her, dress after dress, charms stitched into their bodices with the hair of girls who'd died for love, and these dresses were always wet. A skin does many things. One of those, it seemed, was to hold the dampness in.

Still, he was lucky. She was obedient, this bride. Beautiful and obedient and utterly his. And yet.

And yet.

He shook the thought away like a fly. Like a fly, it came back: a change had recently come over his maiden. No more did she seek to escape him; she followed him instead. No longer did he have to retrieve her; she was always by his side. At night she breathed steadily in his arms, a wakeful kind of breathing that shredded his dreams to restless pieces. When he woke in the deepest hours, he could see the shine of her open eyes. If he believed himself to be alone—in the stables, perhaps, or walking over the grounds—he would turn and find his wife at his elbow, quiet as only a thing of the woods can be quiet. So quickly she'd learned to mute the bellows of her lungs, the ticking of her naked heart. When she found him like this he did not like to look at her, because if he did she would repeat the only words she had spoken since he took her from the woods.

"Give me back my skin."

She said it evenly, without pleading or resentment, but would say nothing else. If she begged, he thought, if she raged, one day he might have complied. But she did not.

The days passed and with them the first fever of his wanting, the heady joy of having won. The day came when the prince grew weary of his maiden. The touch of her gaze was like the stinging of silver insects. He dreaded her silent approach and sensed she had secrets from him still, that hid deeper even than the exposed recesses of her rib cage. Finally he banished her from his chambers, taking comfort, at least in sleep, in the walls of his solitary room.

Still he woke in the night with the sense that someone was watching him. When he lit his lantern, nothing was revealed by its light.

The castle whispered about the prince's unsuitable bride. After the old witch spread the story of their rough courtship, even the servants watched the maiden for signs of savagery. They carried their tales back to the witch: that the girl lived, still, as if she'd never lost her bearskin. That she kept her chambers like a den, the windows covered and the fire unlit. She was starting, they said, to stink. Her chambermaid said worse things yet, claiming the girl had bitten two fingers off a servant who tried to change the sheets on her unused bed. There were rumors, too, that a maid had gone missing, then a cook. But servants were never reliable.

The witch waited impatiently for the maiden to find her skin, knowing what the prince did not: that once she had extracted from him the secret of its hiding spot, she would not suffer him to live. But, after spending her first days as a wife in a fury of searching, the maiden appeared now to be devoted to her husband, remaining by his side from morning to night.

It was curious, very curious. The witch would, she decided, find the thing herself.

"Look beneath the boy's mattress," she murmured to her son. He would make a good king one day, so long as he had his mother at his ear. "Look in the stables, look inside his mother's bridal chest. Try the closets, try the chamber pot, run your fingers over every seam."

The prince had concealed the skin well, but nothing stays hidden forever. The witch put her feet up at night and drank glasses of red liquor, congratulating herself on bringing a bride as good as an assassin's knife into the castle. Once the skin was found, vengeance could not be far behind.

The prince had never been clever, but he was inspired in his concealment of the skin. After he and his maiden were married, he'd climbed to the highest tower, reached out its narrow window, and hooked the thing onto an outcropping of stone. When it rained, she felt a terrible pricking all over her body, as the skin was pelted with drops. When it snowed, she shivered; when the sun beat down, she twisted with the heat.

The maiden suffered under the torment without insight, her animal's mind unsuited to parsing such mysteries. She filled her waking hours as best she could and slept very little, refreshing herself but briefly from her well of deep black dreams. She gave in at times to grief, when no one could see her. But she did that less and less. It was better to live as her animal self had lived, moment to moment, muzzle always reddened by berries or blood. The servants had stopped visiting her rooms, but she knew how to find them. She could creep and slip and let her body become one with the shadows. She never went hungry, those days. But still she longed for her skin.

In time she came to understand a crucial thing. Patience was rewarded in the wild woods. Here, in the castle's polished halls, action was the more certain course.

The prince woke early one morning to find his fire had gone out. No breakfast waited for him, his washing water was stale. He called, then shouted, then became uneasy. He expected his wife to meet him at his door, as she always did, to ask for the return of her skin. But even she was not there.

Your skin, he thought, walking to breakfast. *Your wretched skin*. He didn't know what had woken him so early; the sun was still rising. He'd had too much wine the night before and his mind was moving slowly. Otherwise he might have remarked on the quiet of the castle. He might have found it troubling that half the lamps had gone out, that there were no maids to steer carefully clear of him in the halls.

He was startled to find his father at table. The king hadn't left his chambers in months, and when he did he was never alone. Even when he slept two men stood guard against bad dreams. Odder still was to see the old man looking so lively. Nervously the prince considered that his father could get well, and rule for many years to come.

"Hello, my son." The king's eyes were bright.

The prince bowed first and then recoiled. There was an odor coming off the old man. Gingerly he sat, looking around for a servant to bring him breakfast.

"Closer than that," said the king.

Reluctantly the prince moved to the seat beside his father. There the smell was worse. It was a metallic scent, edged with a dreadful sweetness.

"Closer still," the old man said. "Come kiss your father."

With great distaste the prince leaned toward the king's cheek. As he did so the man turned his head, kissing his son on the mouth with lips that tasted of blood. The prince was too startled to escape him. And with dawning horror he realized that the old man's eyes, though familiar, were not the king's own. They were the eyes of the skinned maiden.

The prince leapt up, alight all over with terror. The lips he had kissed curdled into an awful smile, as his wife slithered free of the king's wet skin. She stood bare before him, and he saw her clearly at last. Not a skinned maiden, but an unsheathed blade.

"I have tried on many skins this night," she said. "Servant skin, witch skin, skin of a king. But none suits me so well as my own. Give me back my skin."

The prince ran. Recklessly at first and then, when reason returned to him, toward the stairs. He stumbled over something lying in the hall—what was left of the witch, her gray-threaded hair still attached at the scalp. He swallowed his bile and ran on.

The sun rose higher, baking the windows and illuminating the awful evidence of his bride's long night. Fear sped his step, and still the maiden outpaced him, meeting him at the top of each stair.

"Give me back my skin," she said.

He reached the tower at the castle's very peak. It was empty but for a spinning wheel with a silver spindle, a piece of his mother's dowry. The maiden watched as he reached through the window and retrieved her skin with trembling fingers.

"Here," he said, thrusting it at her. "Here is your skin. Take it and go."

The maiden seized the thing and tucked it about herself with care. But the skin had been long mistreated, scorched by sun, pummeled with rain, bitten by frost. Her self showed through it in pieces.

"It does not fit me anymore," she said. "I cannot make enough of too little. But"—and she looked toward the spinning wheel—"I can easily make enough of too much."

The prince was fast, but not so fast as a creature of the woods. The maiden girded the gaps in her skin with choice bits taken from her husband's, until she had something that suited her very well. Thus protected, she returned to the woods, and found herself welcome.

ALICE-
THREE-
TIMES

When Alice was born her eyes were black from end to end, and the midwife didn't stay long enough to wash her. After the queen sent the old woman away, she looked a long while at her baby: sallow and placid and long as a tadpole, black eyes washed cool by the sun. The queen had suspected the child was not her husband's, and now she was certain. The baby had the glittering gaze and sullen mouth of the feral people who lived in the ice caves at the very cap of the Hinterland. For a time the king had taken their ruler as his consort, when she and a band of her men visited the castle. In a weak moment the queen revenged herself on her husband with one of these hard-eyed men. This baby was her reward.

The thing was its father's from forehead to heel. Only its hair was the queen's: showing yellow already, enough of it to curl. The queen studied the creature, feeling the places where its passage had unknit her. She thought of the names she could give it, all suitable for a princess, and rejected them. For now, at least, the baby would be nameless.

On her way through the castle the midwife spread the tale of the little princess's birth. She whispered of the girl's black eyes and her silence, and the queen's cold fury at what she had made. In the kitchen she was given a glass of liquor to nurse, and told her story louder:

that the girl had the eyes of the secretive mountain folk. That she left her mother's womb on a gush, not of blood, but of ice water.

Though the queen was not then in favor with her husband, still she had her spies. The midwife remembered that when the knife came down in her cottage that night, silencing her prattling tongue.

The queen slept easier when the midwife was dead, but there was still the matter of the baby to attend to. She was given first to one wet nurse and then another, and neither could feed her. Both claimed the touch of her mouth dried their milk at the source. At last the girl was handed to a servant, who was instructed to raise her on sheep's milk.

The queen would've been glad to hide the baby away, but the king liked to bring the little thing along for hunts and feasts and festivals. Their marriage was ever a warring of two kinds of power, and he enjoyed the queen's shame at this display of her infidelity. Though the court indulged the king and made sport of the queen, no one looked too closely at the child, at her drowning, bead-black eyes. Even the servant who was her nursemaid kept away from her as much as she could.

It was some months before anyone noticed the child was growing no bigger. She drank her milk and slept in her cradle and watched her nursemaid quite alertly, but even her nails refused to grow. Two years bloomed and faded, and she remained a wizened, new-fledged thing, who never cried or cooed or even sighed.

Until the frozen day when the nursemaid shuffled

in with her usual bottle of sheep's milk, and saw something amiss in the shapes of the shadows. Hunched in the crib where a baby should be was a little girl, hair to her shoulders, limbs frail as a frog's. She was naked, the little shift her baby self slept in discarded on the floor. The room smelled of iron and burning hair.

The child fixed her char-colored gaze on the nursemaid and spoke the first words anyone had ever had of her.

"I require new clothes."

For a time the queen's fast-growing bastard was a novelty. A wardrobe was made for her, miniatures of the queen's own clothes, and the nursemaid learned to dress her yellow hair. Courtiers asked her questions and laughed at the precision of her replies, her perfectly formed sentences and the coolness with which she considered the world. *Would you like a lovely doll? No, I would not. What would you have instead? That jewel just there, on your hand. Give it to me.* They laughed, but they shivered, too. To have the princess look at you too long was a feeling akin to dipping your hand in cold oil. It was hard, afterward, to remove the feel of it.

Since the girl's birth the marriage of the king and queen had passed through many seasons—cool, warm, frigid, blistering. During their periods of good understanding, the queen conceived again twice. One child she carried in her arms, the other in her belly. When she looked at her black-eyed brat, she knew by instinct to hold the baby closer, to curl an arm over her stomach.

The king pressed her to finally give a name to the bastard girl, and the queen considered it. How the thing you're called could shape your road.

She chose a small, ill-starred name, not fit for royalty. A name with a wish inside it: that the little girl would not outlive her childhood. The queen called her Alice.

Soon the court's changeable attentions turned away from Alice and toward the next bright thing. She was no longer coddled or delighted in, and drifted away from the life of the castle.

She preferred being left to her own devices. Her nursemaid was negligent at best, and as the months passed the princess's new clothes grew ragged. When summer came she shunned the sun, hiding in the castle's coolest chambers. When it grew cold again, she slid through the shadows, over the lawns, frightening the maids and making her siblings cry just by looking at them. She never outgrew her dresses, never grew at all, and in time the castle forgot her feat of leaving babyhood behind overnight.

Then, on a breath-freezing morning many months after the princess cast off her infant self, she performed the trick once more. Overnight she became a black-eyed girl of twelve, a coltish creature of angles and points who could barely walk on her new legs. When the queen heard what had happened, she had her daughter brought before her.

The queen by then had borne six children, three before Alice and two after. She'd been a bride at sixteen and was nearly thirty, and still she was small as a girl, her yellow hair falling past her hips.

She looked at Alice from atop her throne. Descending, she circled the child, pinching bruises onto her skin, squeezing her chin in her nails, staring as long as she could stand it into her eyes. She tugged sharply on her daughter's hair, so like her own. Alice's nursemaid stood in the doorway, unsure what she should do if the queen decided to kill her charge.

I mustn't help her do it, the nursemaid thought. *But nor would I stop her.*

The queen didn't kill her daughter, though later she had cause to regret it. When she spoke, it wasn't to Alice.

"Hire another servant to watch her," she told the nursemaid. "Hire two. And be sure my children are never left alone with her. Be sure they're never left alone at all."

As she wished it, so it was done. But still Alice found her way to the queen's other children. The younger ones bore odd-shaped bruises in hidden places, while the elder grew thin on a diet of strange dreams, violent in their beauty: of ice that glistened like gemstones and frozen dancing halls carved deep beneath the earth, where men with jet-colored eyes offered their calloused hands. Without knowing it, the castle held its breath, everyone listening with one ear for Alice's approach—her sliding step, the bounce of her silver ball. Servants left in the night, and members of the court spoke of finding marks on their skin any place the princess's eye had touched. A lord might see her in the gallery, and a lady in the music room, and later discover they'd seen her at the same moment. She was never seen moving anything but slowly, yet seemed to travel too quick.

When the queen threw herself on her husband's mercy, begging for Alice's exile, he was receptive to her pleas. He would, he told her, send the girl out into the world the very next day. With her would go her nursemaid, a carriage, two horses, and a purse of gold. What became of her after that was nobody's concern but her own.

When the nursemaid heard of the king's plans, she grew bitter. Years of her life she'd spent in the keeping of a loveless child; would she spend the rest of it in exile?

She would not. She would use poison to ensure it. Her only consideration was whether to kill the princess now, before they left the castle, or to take her chances on the road, where she could claim the king's carriage and purse of gold as her own. By the morning's earliest hour she'd made her decision. She would kill the girl now. Even if she were caught, she reasoned, the queen would intercede on her behalf. No one would be punished for bringing about the death of this Alice.

The nursemaid carried a tray that held the princess's breakfast: a bowl of chipped, honey-sweetened ice and a carafe of watered wine, both sprinkled liberally with a flavorless poison.

But from the hallway she caught again the awful odor that marked the girl's previous changes—the sick-room scent of spilled blood, of bones broken and reset. Her feet faltered, the tray rattled in her hands.

Waiting for her in Alice's bed was a girl of seventeen. Her hair was as long as the queen's, her black eyes set like two faceted stones. The princess, now three times grown, blinked at the woman on whose indifference she had been raised. It was the slow, cold blink of a slow, cold heart.

"You may leave my service at once," the princess said. "Or you may sit beside me and eat my breakfast yourself."

The nursemaid was not seen in the castle after that day.

The queen woke the morning of Alice's exile with a light heart and a heavy head, foggy with the tincture she drank each night to stop her from dreaming. She was a long time in preparing herself to sit beside the king as he banished the wicked girl. Her hair was dressed in opals and thin-hammered coins. Her gown was cloth of gold. Her livid lips were painted over in white and her lashes blackened. She smiled to see herself looking as she did when she was a merchant's daughter standing in the snow, catching the eye of a king. She was pregnant again, though only she knew it. She let her dress drape itself over the first swelling of her stomach.

In the throne room the king was already in his seat, the court lined up before him. The air was laced with the scent of smelted iron, singed hair. The courtiers cast covert glances toward the queen as she entered, and whispered behind their hands.

A girl stood before the king. Her skin shone like nacre around a ragged dress, too small, and her hair fell over her back in dense yellow waves. The queen had forgotten over their many married years how the king had looked at her when she was a girl and he newly crowned and their marriage date just set. He was looking in just that way at this girl, this blond-and-pearl stranger.

The stranger turned as the queen approached. Her eyes held and swallowed the light, so that over her face there hovered a darkness. They were black from end to end.

Even the king's closest confidants, even his most rapacious companions, attempted to dissuade him from courting the queen's bastard.

"She is not my own child," he told his counselors. "I will not be moved. And since when does a king explain himself?"

Alice's exile was forgotten. As the queen thickened with her seventh pregnancy, the king held feasts and dances in Alice's honor. He gave her gifts not meant for a daughter: a dragonfly catch for her cloak, made of red metal. A blown-glass flower that looked like a scorpion striking. Sculptures carved of ice, before which she stood enchanted. Though she gave no other sign of softening toward her mother's husband, her indifference only inflamed his passion. The court said that the girl had bewitched him.

As for Alice, no one could say how her thoughts might run. But as the king's courtship stretched on, the castle fell under a spell of bad luck. The queen blamed all of it on the girl: the dark dreams that stalked the court, the unexplained deaths of the stable's best horses, the hysteria that overtook the servants like a plague, coming and going in a fortnight. Spoiled milk, bad weather. The obsession of the king.

It struck the queen that the girl could be working out of desperation, seeking escape from royal courtship. The idea came and went. She could not learn this late to pity Alice.

One night the queen fell asleep before she could give her children the drafts that sent them to a place deeper than dreaming, protecting them from the visions she feared Alice might plant in their heads. She woke in the dark with a pounding heart.

The queen took up a candle. Barefoot and trembling, she moved through her children's rooms, holding the candle aloft to see each beloved face, softened by sleep. One, two, three, four, all of them breathing quietly. But the fifth bed, where her second son slept, was empty, its coverlet folded back. Alice, too, was missing from her chamber.

Alice returned by morning. The queen's son did not. The servants meant to protect the one from the other were hanged, but Alice remained under the king's protection.

"You cannot prove it," he said, "and he may yet come home. This grudge has made you foolish."

The queen could not have the girl killed. She could not exile her. She could not hold her head underwater until her black eyes closed. Forced to find a more palatable means of getting rid of her, and heedless of the king's desires, she decreed the girl's eligibility for marriage.

The rules she set were this: Alice would be given to the first man who would have her. If he were poor or cruel or both together, all the better.

Though the king raged when he learned of it, the declaration had been made. The suitors came, among them both princes and paupers. But Alice would not look at them. She who dealt her words as carefully as cards now made her own decree.

"Ice," she said. "I will marry the first man to bring me a silk purse filled to the brim with it. Not just any ice, but that which is found in the caverns at the top of the world. Those who try and fail must lose their lives."

The girl was a bastard and a monstrosity, but she was also a princess, and her words had weight. While no royal maiden could refuse to marry, any could set the terms by which her hand was won.

Now the suitors came armed against her request,

and proved themselves foolish. Some brought ice that melted to water along the way. Some carried great harvested slabs of it from the king's own stream. Some presented diamonds to frost the princess's fingers and throat, and learned too late her request was not a metaphor. The days went by, the suitors failed and fell, and the queen despaired of the girl ever marrying.

Until, on a raw spring day, two brothers arrived on foot. Their clothing was threadbare, their ruddy hair dark with sweat. Each carried a crate in his arms.

The jostling pack of courtiers and other suitors laughed at the ill-dressed men. The brothers ignored them, walking with laden arms to where Alice sat between the king and the queen. Behind her stood her father's headswoman, who struggled to keep her ax clean between executions. The brothers dropped their crates at Alice's feet and pried them open.

First came the lights. Cast from the open crates, they played like moving constellations over the walls and the distant ceiling, the crowd of suddenly solemn faces. The queen's heart lightened and lifted, the king's darkened and dropped. Alice's fingers squeezed bloodless around her skirts.

From each crate the brothers hefted a block of ice, brushing away the sawdust it was packed in. Every eye was drawn to it, everyone who saw it remembered a dream they'd had once, for good or for ill. The ice was glass-clear in places and silvered with bubbles in others. In it swam lights of green and violet and palest pink, always moving, tugging the hearts of those who saw it upward, toward the caverns from whence it had come. Many a suitor sighed as the brothers took out carving knives and cut a block into pieces.

Alice stood silent as the older brother counted chunks of ice into a velvet purse. There was a singing in her head: the high, thin whine ice makes when it softens. She'd never heard it before, but was born knowing its sound. The men who had won her stood at her feet, but she had eyes only for the ice.

"Which one of you will she marry?" the king asked, his voice churlish.

"I don't want a wife," said the older brother. "I want to bring a princess low. She'll bake our bread and clean our house and bear the children who will serve us after she's dead."

The queen's white-painted lips parted in an unseemly smile. Even the king seemed disconcerted by it. But Alice didn't look at her mother, or the men. She held the purse of ice to her lips and tipped it down her throat.

Those nearest to her could hear the princess's sigh of contentment before the frost overtook her. It crawled over her lips, it bloomed over her limbs. Her skin went blue, her eyes iced over, and she dropped softly to the ground, a frozen maiden wrapped in her own yellow hair.

The gathered court sprang back in case the cold was catching. The queen cried out, one high, fierce note of triumph, and the elder brother shouted with dismay over his fallen prize. He quarreled for a time with the king, till it was decided he would take the princess as she was, and decide her fate on the road.

The brothers set off that night, Alice tied to the back of a horse the king gave as her dowry. The queen watched her go, waiting for the sliver of ice that lodged beside her heart to melt away.

The brothers rode until the stars faded, then stopped to make camp. They laid their bedrolls on the ground and their princess beneath a tree. The elder brother fell easily into a heavy sleep, but the younger twisted in the grip of terrible dreams, of a white-furred fox with holes for eyes and a child who laughed while drowning in an icy pond. Of the things they'd seen while harvesting Alice's ice.

As the sun bled over the horizon, he woke to find his brother unmoving beside him. The dead man's skin bristled with frost, his eyes were frozen wide. The younger brother sprang to his feet, looking toward the princess.

She lay where they'd left her. When he kicked her with his boot, she did not move.

The man thought fast. He tied Alice's hands and feet with strong rope and quickly packed up camp. Leaving the princess behind with his dead brother, he rode away like Death was after him.

It was not winter, but he heard wintry sounds as he went: the wind through frozen branches, gouts of wet snow thumping to the ground. He spurred his horse faster. When the animal was covered in froth and the brother too exhausted to continue, he made camp. All night he held a knife at the ready, keeping a fire alive and a lookout over the road. When nothing had come for him by dawn, he began to feel foolish.

Until the rising sun illuminated his horse. The dead animal's eyes were covered with a membrane of frost and its mane was hung with ice crystals. There were tracks leading to it in the snow. Not footprints, but the trail of something that slid.

The younger brother fled. In his terror he found his way into the deepest part of the forest, where the air froze his throat and chilled his eyes until they ached. It was twilight when he collapsed, so tired he couldn't summon the strength to feel afraid.

When he was asleep, the princess crept out from behind a tree hung with vines. She knelt over the brother and cupped her hands to his face. She placed her mouth on his.

When he was dead, Alice stood up tall. The ice was moving in her, swirling in her eyes like cirrus clouds. On the wind she caught the breath of cold lilacs, a late freeze on an early bloom. It was the scent of her mother's perfume. When she closed her eyes she could feel the faraway queen, the pulse of her triumphant heart.

The queen's victory did not sate her.

Her son was still gone. The king still longed for the departed princess, even more beautiful in memory than in his halls. There were still the dead to be seen to, a battlefield's worth of fallen suitors, and her own injured pride.

And, she thought that night, lying sleepless in her chambers, there was the remaining block of ice. The brothers who took Alice had carved only one.

She walked on bare feet to the throne room. The whole place shifted with the ice's delicate lights, so it felt as if she walked underwater. The queen circled the block, closer and closer, the chill breathing from its sides dusting goose bumps over her skin.

What had her daughter felt when she swallowed the ice?

She shook the word away—*daughter*—but the feeling of it stayed.

Kneeling beside the block, she pressed her palms to its side. She leaned in to touch her tongue to it, so she might know the taste. Before she could, something shifted in its depths. The ice fogged then bubbled then went clear as a mirror, showing not the queen's face but Alice's.

The queen looked into the ice that had become a scrying glass. She held her breath.

Alice walked, her shadow dragging behind her like a woman's black hair. She moved past villages full of sleepers whose eyes stretched sudden in the dark, through woods full of hungry creatures who cringed at her passing. Everywhere she stepped her footfall sowed some dark thing: premonitions and killing frost, seedlings that strangled.

Growing weary, the girl lay beneath a row of acanthus,

*closing her eyes and dropping into a rest that was less like
sleep than stillness. The sun rose and the acanthus wept their
heavy lobes and the bees that drowsed over them fell like
golden rain, poisoned by the girl's frozen breath.*

*After a time the princess woke. Rose to her feet. With a
coal-colored gaze she looked at the queen, and smiled.*

The queen fell back onto the throne room's hard
floor. Her body was stiff. The lantern she'd placed beside herself was out.

When she looked again at the ice, the vision had
wiped itself away. But she knew the part of the woods
where Alice slept. It lay on her own land.

The queen wrapped herself in furs and ascended the
castle's many stairs, climbing to its highest parapet.
There was a ticking in her belly where once the infant
Alice had seized and swum. She watched as, far below,
travelers left and entered the woods. Carts trundled
noiselessly over the dirt. The smoke of a distant village
turned to haze.

A figure stepped from the trees, onto the road.

The queen's eyes blurred. For a moment it seemed
there were three figures looking up at her, too far to
see yet she knew them anyway, knew they watched her,
too. When she blinked they snapped into the shape of
a single girl.

The queen's life moved in her a little longer yet. Anything might happen. Any tale could be true. She whispered this to herself, the words dropping like diamonds
and rattlesnakes from her whitened lips.

Down there, on the road, Alice's mouth moved, too.

The queen did not know what stories she told herself, what new endings she might devise.

It's not everyone who gets to see their death as it comes. The queen waited for the future, for the end. The cold was already in her.

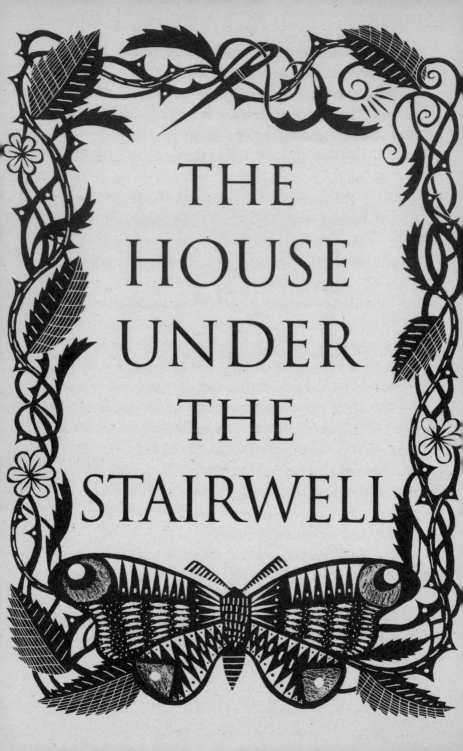

THE
HOUSE
UNDER
THE
STAIRWELL

On a knife-bright day at the edge of an overgrown garden, three sisters pricked their fingers on a briar and let their blood fall to the earth.

Below the briar, it was said, lay the body of a bride who died on her wedding night. She was called the Wicked Wife. If you let your blood drop over the briar that covered her grave, she came to you in dreams to share a vision of the one you'd marry.

The eldest of the sisters, Isobel, had suffered a broken engagement. In her eagerness to forget the man she loved, she became determined to visit the grave, and her sisters followed after. As their blood disappeared into the briar, the first cold breath of winter came from the mouth of the woods, snow rattling in it like loose teeth. The girls shivered, drawing bloody fingers into their cloaks, and turned their backs to the trees.

That night, tucked up in bed, they dreamed.

The youngest sister smiled over a breakfast table at a man with wise eyes, strong hands, and a rambling house filled with beautiful things.

The middle sister walked with a broad-shouldered man through an orchard. He plucked a fruit off a pear tree and gave it to her.

Isobel had a stranger dream.

As her sisters smiled in their sleep, she fretted and turned, her pillow too hot and her blankets stifling. In the days since her jilting, she'd dreamed only of the man who'd humiliated her. Would she fall asleep tonight and dream of him still? After a long restless time, she left her bed and moved to the window. There she watched the snow fall, running the fingers of one hand over the place on the other where an engagement ring had sat.

When she turned from the window, a woman stood between her and her bed. Moonlight ran through the woman in a thousand silver spearpoints. Her hair was red, her dress was white, her neck was crooked. She wore a wooden mask painted with the golden face of a lioness.

"You wish to hear of your husband?" Her voice made a cold music. The shush of wind in bare branches, the tapping of a dead girl's wedding shoes.

"Am I asleep?" Isobel whispered. "Are you the Wicked Wife?"

Shadows shaped like fingers crawled up the woman's skirts; she shook them away. "You wish to hear of your husband?" she said once more. "I'll take you to meet him this very night."

From behind Isobel came a hissing giggle, like cold water on hot coals, and two figures moved to flank her. They were small as children and oddly hunched, their bodies dressed in yellow. They, too, wore wooden masks, painted with the faces of beautiful girls.

Isobel looked at their curving backs and the ears that twitched over the tops of their masks, fox-red and pointed. She looked at the mournful column of the white-dressed bride and thought of her lost fiancé, set to marry a girl he'd just met.

"Take me to my husband," she said.

The fox girls bobbed around her, chittering with laughter. They ran a bitten berry over her lips and slipped satin dancing shoes onto her feet. Then they led her from the room, down the hall, to an unfamiliar stair.

Its steps were polished stone, descending past walls hung with paintings rich as marzipan, where ladies danced in gilded rooms and gentlemen hunted in jeweled forests. Isobel walked down and down, until her feet ached. The stairs ended at last in the middle of a rambling moor covered thickly with snow.

There was no sky here, but a roof of earth, heavy coils of roots running through it. Moths larger than men perched on the roots with their wings open wide, casting a delicate glow. In the distance stood a house with lights shining through every window, and before it a grove of gold and silver trees. A masked figure waited beneath each tree, limbs too long and fingers hidden in dark gloves. Above their masks, each painted with a man's face, stood wiry gray wolf ears. The nearest bowed to Isobel and offered his hand.

I am dreaming, she told herself as she took it. *I am fast asleep.*

The wolf-eared dancers spun her about the grove, passing her from one to the next. The snow bloomed red as her slippers shredded and her bare feet bloodied themselves on the points of fallen leaves. Snowflakes fell from the metal trees, clotting in her lashes and melting on her tongue.

Dizzy with dancing and the pain in her feet, Isobel caught herself against the chest of a figure taller than the rest. The eyes behind his mask were amber around a dull black pupil, his ears tawny as a cat's. His arms came around her, gloved fingers pressing bruises into the small of her back. The scent of him was old bed-clothes and vetiver.

Beneath the drifting snowflakes, bathed in pale mothlight, they danced. After a time he dipped his mouth to her ear.

"What heartbreak are you running from, that you've found your way to me? Happy women do not walk beneath the stairwell."

His voice made every part of her prickle with cold caution. "My heartbreak is not so great," she said faintly. "When I wake from this dream, it will be half healed."

The lion-eyed figure laughed, an awful rumble that ran below his skin and caught behind the unyielding smile of his mask. "Do you pretend even now that you're sleeping? Here, let me wake you up."

Pain burst in her back, ten fine points of it, as he flexed fierce claws that stabbed and retreated. She gasped and staggered, and would have fallen if he did not hold her up, still turning, still moving her body through the dance.

"I think we understand each other now," he murmured. "So hear this. All you see beneath the stairwell belongs to me, every stone and stick of it. Passing into my lands is free. It's leaving them that comes with a cost."

It took Isobel three tries to catch her breath. "What cost?"

"Your hand in marriage."

"A high toll for one dance."

"Be patient, my unhappy love. We'll do more than dance on our wedding night."

He spun her once more about his moth-lit dreamland, his trap baited with tales of the Wicked Wife. When he let her go, she stumbled to her knees, looking up at his shape traced against the earthen sky.

His voice mocked her as he turned away. "Hurry, my love, back to your maiden's bed. I'll claim you one year hence, when the winter's first snow falls."

The wolf-men were gone, and the fox-eared girls in their yellow clothes. Far overhead, the moths swooped like bats through the growing dark. The shining form of the Wicked Wife reappeared among the trees to hurry Isobel through the grove, over the moor, up and up the stairs.

Pain glittered in her back and feet. The ghost's nearness chilled her; she felt half sick with cold when at last they reached the threshold of home. Her room was dark and smelled of ashes, and her sisters were lost to different dreams, which made them cry out in their sleep.

She fell into bed, her head a wilderness of briars

and mothlight and masked men. The Wicked Wife lingered beside her, a shape almost lost in the brightening dark.

Through a scrim of exhaustion, Isobel spoke.

"What manner of monster are you, to lead me to that place?"

The dead bride drifted a while before speaking. "One made by the acts of men."

"I won't marry him," the girl murmured, already halfway to sleep.

"You will," the ghost replied. "We always do."

She stayed for a time, as Isobel slept.

Poor girl, she sighed. *Poor girl, poor girl.*

Perhaps she was speaking of herself.

In the morning the youngest sister boasted of the rich man she'd met in her dreams. The middle sister spoke more quietly, of her husband-to-be's handsome face and strong arms. When it was Isobel's turn, she told her sisters her sleep had been dreamless.

"I suppose you'll never marry," said the youngest, her face soft with pity.

Isobel curled bloody toes beneath her blankets. Fiercely, she wished it to be true.

Isobel burned the satin slippers. Her battered feet reknit themselves. But she could not forgive herself so easily. She was an eldest sister, and still she'd gotten herself caught in some creature's net.

Away from the world beneath the stairwell, she began to calculate. She'd given no promises, she told herself. She'd eaten nothing, kissed no one. All she'd done was dance.

But all that winter, the grove and the suitor's threats held her in their grip. Her sleep was unsettled, opaque. She could not descend the stairs without an ache in her feet and a rising dread. She found herself misplacing things: a copper thimble, a bracelet of braided metal. A blue glove embroidered with darker blue forget-me-nots.

Her distraction lasted until spring. The season's first green breath brought her back to herself, infected her with an appetite for open air. Perhaps, she ventured to hope, her night beneath the stairwell had never really happened. The Wicked Wife was just a tale, after all.

Then her youngest sister came home from a dinner party with flushed cheeks. She gathered her sisters close and revealed that she'd met him, the man from her dream. She'd known him at once. He was as rich and handsome as she remembered, and he'd spent the entire evening by her side.

The next day the man presented himself, speaking to their father before putting a ring on the girl's hand. Isobel blanched, and smiled, and congratulated her sister.

Soon after that, the middle sister spied the man she'd seen in dreams at a market day. He wrapped her finger in a flower stem and promised a ring would come.

Isobel wished her well in a voice frail as paper. And when she could manage it, she slipped away, back to the abandoned garden where briars grew over the grave of the Wicked Wife.

She paced among them, catching her skirts on their teeth and disturbing the bees. She was in danger, or she was a fool. She was cursed, or she was hunted by nothing but a night of dark dreaming. With one foot she walked a solid path, while the other trod in nightmare. She did not know which to believe in.

Nothing for it but to take the knife from her boot, let it bite her finger, and watch her blood drop onto the briar.

What a fool I've become, she lamented, *to court a phantom twice.*

But her sleep that night was dreamless, as deep and dark as the sea. She rose from it with aching eyes.

On the pillow beside her lay a wooden mask. It was carved from oak, its painted tiger stripes garish in the sun. Softly she lifted the thing, feeling its clumsy weight. Then she tossed it onto the fire.

It was better to know, she told herself, as the flames washed it to ash. Better than to waste her time in wondering.

Her youngest sister's wedding was set for the very start of summer. When she woke on the day of the festivities, Isobel set her troubles aside. Tomorrow she would worry and scheme. Today she would smile and weep only happy tears. She would dress in green satin and lay a wreath of hellebore in her hair.

She was watching the wedding party with a pinned-on smile when a young man approached her.

He was a cousin of the groom, with the same warm eyes and green-rinsed hair; she'd heard it said that their mothers' mother had been scooped by her husband from the sea.

He held out a hand. "Will you dance?"

Isobel hadn't danced since the night her broken feet painted roses over the snow. But she let him lead her into the crowd, counting her quickening breaths as they spun. Smiling back when he pulled a blossom from her hair and kissed it. Laughing when he lifted her in tandem with the other dancers, his hands on her waist light as water.

She danced with him a second time, a third. *I could do it,* she thought. Letting him brush his lips over her fingers, then her palm, then her mouth. It would be no hardship to let this man win her. He was finely made, he stood solid on the earth. And he could protect her from other entanglements. When the suitor from below the stairwell came to claim her, she would show him another man's ring on her finger. No one need know she'd nearly been tricked into giving herself away.

All went as she hoped. The young man visited her the day after the wedding, and every day after that. He was the son of a shipwright, with a quick laugh and gentle manners, easy to like. When he asked for her hand, she gave it to him gladly, feeling her neck slip free of the noose.

In her father's hall they toasted the engagement. Late that night, tipsy and triumphant, she ascended the stairs alone.

Did she imagine the shadows that lay drift-deep beneath each step? Were there more stairs than there ought to be, carrying her up and up until, panting, she reached the landing at last?

In her room she moved quickly to the mirror, finding in it her hand and its engagement ring. Her breathing settled as she looked at the ring's reflection, lifting her fingers to admire its light.

Inside the mirror's watery oval, the stone wriggled from its setting. It shuddered and stretched damp wings, becoming a pale moth that rose to tangle itself in her hair.

When her mother rushed in, drawn by Isobel's screams, she found her daughter doubled over, clawing at her head. There was nothing there that the older woman could see. The engagement ring shone, unchanged, from her daughter's finger.

Isobel told her betrothed they must be married at once. That very day. He said it was impossible: he and his father must sail down the coast to deliver a ship to a king. He would travel home on horseback, in time for them to be wed before winter.

"Return to me before the first snow falls," she told him, "or it will go badly for us."

He smiled to soothe her worries, kissed her, and went away. In the quiet left by his absence she learned he was more than an escape from a tightening knot: she had come to love him.

But her love was harried by the suitor below the

stairs. Unseen hands left moldering roses on her pillow. The ivory skeleton of a songbird appeared in pieces at the bottom of her soup bowl. One night she woke to the sound of hissing laughter and the phantom feeling of fingers on her skin, and found a necklace of woven metal branches wrapped tightly around her throat.

She suffered without speaking and her family smiled to see it, calling her lovesick.

Summer ripened, then rotted. The heat broke and it was autumn. With the new season came a dead weasel at the foot of her bed, its long body wrapped in white satin. A fox's paw in her left dancing shoe. She disposed of the weasel, threw the paw on the fire. The leaves crackled into sunburn colors and the preparations for her wedding to the shipwright's son heightened. On the day her bridal dress was delivered, a rat's gray pelt fell from its folds.

At last she received word from her betrothed that he was on his way home. Business had gone better than expected, they could be married without delay.

It was autumn still. Late autumn but warm, the skies clear and freckled with the falling bodies of leaves. She would marry her love before the snow fell, and be safe.

Their wedding day dawned pale. The clouds' bellies hung low and the breezes blew cold. Isobel's mother lit lamps, chiding her daughter for standing at the window watching the sky.

The wedding guests arrived and Isobel was dressed in white lace, made to move among them. Whenever she could, she looked out at the yard. It was nearly dark when her fiancé arrived on the back of a steaming horse. She ran to him, her dress dragging behind her.

Muddy-hemmed and panting, she reached up to seize his hands. Before they could touch, the clouds gave way, letting fall the winter's first snow.

Quickly, quickly. Isobel pulled him through the yard, into the house, past their drunken guests. He was laughing at first, then not, as she led him to the judge, who sat with a wineglass in one hand and a cake plate on his knee.

"Marry us," she told him.

"My mother isn't here yet," protested her fiancé.

"I must finish my wine," the judge said sourly.

A knocking came at the door.

"Perhaps that's my mother now," her betrothed murmured.

The judge swallowed the last of his drink.

"Stop!" Isobel cried, but her father was already opening the door.

Through it came a crowd of figures in bridesmaids' gowns, their hands gloved and their slippers trailing yellow ribbons. Their wooden masks were painted with joyful faces and circlets of lilies crowned their pointed ears. One bridesmaid was dressed more lavishly than the rest, in velvet adorned with tiny mirrors that threw sequins of light over the guests. She walked to the room's center, lifted a fiddle to her chin, and began to play.

The music wound round the guests like piano wire. Though Isobel tugged at the hands of her betrothed and the arms of her sisters, though she pleaded in her mother's ear, they would not look at her. They only gazed at the masked girls dancing prettily as marionettes.

The fiddler's song spun wilder, till the wedding party's entrancement turned to toes tapping and the fox girls whirled among the guests, drawing them into the dance. When the fiddler dropped her instrument, the thing played itself, perched against empty air as she took the hands of the bridegroom.

Isobel stood alone in a room swaying with masked dancers and smiling guests. They were drunk and glad; they laughed with pleasure right up until the moment the bridesmaids pulled off their masks, revealing the pointed faces of foxes, and used their shining teeth to rip out the wedding guests' throats.

Off came their heads! They looked happy as they fell but surprised when they landed. Isobel rushed to where her beloved's head had fallen. She leaned down to kiss its lips, weeping as the fox girls seized her up and carried her away.

The long staircase was not as she remembered it. Gone were its polished steps, given way to rough wooden boards weeping splinters. The paintings were transformed: now the women in them consorted with long-tailed beasts, and the men carried their own skins over their shoulders. The gold and silver grove had become a thornwood that tore at Isobel's skin and hair and wedding dress. When they reached the house beyond the woods, her dress was in rags.

The once beautiful house was a ruin, its hall scattered with the bones of small creatures and its ceilings porous as cheese. The fox girls bore the bride to a dusty room where a wooden altar waited. Its boards were stained, and the brown snail curl of a dried orange blossom clung to its front.

"Make your preparations," said the fox girl in the mirrored gown. "Your husband-to-be is on his way."

Isobel held up trembling hands still stained with her fiancé's blood. "If he tries to keep me, I swear by my eyes I will make his life a torment."

The fox *tsk*ed scornfully. "You'll only be his bride of an hour. It's not your company he longs for, it's your blood. Just as flowers wilt for want of water, this house and its grounds thirst and fade without maidens' blood. It is my master's fancy to seduce and marry its meals. After his realm feasts on you it will return, for another year, to its splendor."

The fox laughed its coarse laugh, showing the blood caught on its pointed teeth. All the foxes had shed their wedding clothes; now they dropped to the floor and trotted away, locking the door behind them.

When they were gone, Isobel rattled the door. She stood on her toes to peer out the narrow windows. When she looked back toward the altar, a woman was sitting there. White-dressed and russet-haired, turning her golden lioness mask in filmy fingers.

"I will wait with you," said the Wicked Wife. "Until he comes."

Isobel could not speak above a whisper. "You are to blame for this. You, the Wicked Wife."

"I was a wife, it's true. His very first. But it's only in the mouths of tale tellers that I've become wicked."

"You baited me. You gave me to him."

The ghost's bent neck spoke regret, but her voice was steady. "I was the bait only. Not the hook."

"Then help me. Don't wait with me for death to come, let me escape it."

The ghostly bride opened her mouth as if to speak but, flickering, did not. Instead, her misty body drew in on itself. It shrank into the form of a white dagger, which darted toward the door and rattled through the rusty keyhole, shaking the wood in its frame.

When Isobel tried the door again, she found it unlocked. Alone, she wandered through her suitor's house.

It was like the carcass of a dead beast, its rancid rooms picked rib cages or the chambers of a broken heart. As she walked through a ballroom with blackened walls, Isobel spied a column of ghostly light.

The Wicked Wife hooked a finger at her to follow.

She trailed the ghost through rooms that bubbled with decay, to a staircase made of cloudy rose quartz. The living bride followed the dead one up the stairs, stepping over the places where they'd crumbled. They ended in a door that opened onto a large chamber.

Isobel knew by its odor of dirty sheets and vetiver that it belonged to the suitor. Instead of a bed, there was a nest of silken pelts. A mirror hung on a hook, and on a hatstand a wardrobe of wooden masks, each painted with a different face. Against one wall an enormous bound chest was held in place by roots spangling down through the ceiling.

Isobel trembled to think what might lie inside it. But when she lifted the lid, she saw neither bloody flesh nor cracked bone. The chest was full of trinkets, some so old they were nearly dust, and some quite new. A carding comb, a cloak of gray wool, a needle stuck into a spool of thread. A little clockwork cat with three tails. The withered crown of hellebore made her pause, but it wasn't until she saw her own braided bracelet and vanished blue glove that she understood.

They were keepsakes. Trophies, perhaps. Of Isobel and all the brides who'd come before her.

She closed her weary eyes. The hungry house breathed around her, so certain it had her in its grasp. And she remembered a far-off day, when three sisters let their blood feed a sleeping briar.

Seeds, she thought. All the stolen oddments planted in this chest, they were seeds. The roots that grew from the chest burrowed through an acre of earth and into a wild garden, where they showed their faces as a thicket of briars. *This* was the grave of the Wicked Wife, of all the wicked suitor's blameless wives, planted with the things they'd once held dear.

The blood that warmed her cheeks seemed to speak to her, or maybe it was the Wicked Wife who whispered in her ear: *Let loose your blood. Bleed into this chest as you did on the briars.*

The needle in its spool of thread winked at her. Isobel took it up and stuck it into the tips of her fingers, letting her blood fall onto the contents of the open chest.

As the blood dripped down, she heard a growling from below.

As the things in the chest drank it up, there came a heavy footstep on the stair.

As the stolen trinkets shuddered, a great howling came from outside the door.

The suitor bounded into the room, crouched like a beast in a torn velvet coat. When he flung aside his mask he had a lion's face, pupils drawn tight and dried blood on his muzzle. He made to leap at Isobel, but it was too late.

From each trinket sprang a ghost. With broken bones and blood-silvered throats and chests carved hollow, their eyes glistening like gems in a wedding ring. They smiled at the bristling lion, their teeth, for a moment, sharp as foxes'. Then they descended, their dead hands given form by Isobel's blood.

She watched as the brides took their revenge. From below came the howling of the fox girls, as a host of brides darted down the steps to make short work of them, too.

In the quiet that followed this bloody time, the ghosts gathered around Isobel.

Take my cloak, said one.

Take my key, said another.

Take my needle and thread, whispered a third. *It is not too late.*

And they evanesced into the fragrant air. When the last had disappeared, a rumbling shook the room. From the chest Isobel seized the needle and thread, the cloak, and the key, and fled.

The house went to pieces as she ran. The cloak protected her from all manner of disaster, falling masonry and fast-crawling rot and devouring lines of blue fire. When she reached the house's front door, the key unlocked it.

Fast through the thornwood, her cloak blunting its attack, and up the staircase. All the people in the paintings were dead, the steps scorched dark. When Isobel reached her own front hall, the carnage of her wedding party awaited.

She walked among the broken bodies. Her mother and father. Her sisters in their gowns. Her betrothed with his sea-washed hair. She set aside her grief and picked up the needle and thread.

It took a long time to fit each head to its proper body. It took longer to sew them back on. Her fingers slipped and the needle pierced her and her blood mixed with the blood of the dead. She worked in awful solitude for a day and a night, shuddering to think she might run out of thread. As the sun rose on the second morning after what should have been her wedding day, she used the last inch of it to sew up the throat of the judge.

A wedding party of stitch-necked bodies lay about her, limbs slack and mouths silent. She did not know what came next. The dead brides had given her no instructions.

She thought a while, then kneeled over her betrothed and pressed her cracked lips to his. A moment passed, still as stone. Then he breathed, and sighed, and cried out. From all around them came the shouts of awakening wedding guests, who remembered nothing after the flash of fox eyes, the sudden tearing of flesh.

Wrapped in bloodied finery, by the light of the season's first snow, Isobel and her beloved were wed. The stitches over his throat remained forever as a symbol of his wife's devotion, and her own thornwood scars never quite faded, as a reminder not to trust the touch of a masked man.

ILSA
WAITS

In a village where a plague called the dream sickness slipped from house to house, a man lay dying.

But never a man so young, his wife said, watching the sleeper like she could hold him there just by looking. *The dreaming sickness only takes old men.* Yet the hours passed and still he did not wake.

The dying man had six sons and a daughter named Ilsa, the youngest child and often overlooked. With curious eyes that saw much and understood little, she watched his decline.

The sickroom smelled of dried sweat and burning wood and there were always too many people in it—Ilsa's mother and brothers and the herb-woman who could do nothing but took her coin anyway, just for bathing the dreamer's face in scented water. At the end, as her mother's whispering became a keen and the herb-woman shook her head and six sons moved in to say their goodbyes, Ilsa saw a man she did not know.

There was no such thing as a stranger in the girl's small world, in her hard, poor village tucked among the trees. But she would have remembered this man, whose shape was cut like paper against the room's sour shadows. He sat perfectly still, hands resting on his knees. His pale eyes were on her father.

The dying man's breath labored and slowed. Someone pushed Ilsa toward him, and she went reluctantly.

She didn't know her father well. He was a deep voice in the dark before dawn. A hand on her hair, too hard to be affectionate. But her mother was watching, so Ilsa put her lips to his damp cheek.

When she straightened, the stranger was looking at her.

"Do you see me, child?" His voice was low and slow. His lips were lovely, for a man's.

"Yes," she said, uncertain.

His head tilted. Even that small movement seemed grand. "And yet it is not your time. I think you see too much, little Ilsa."

This was the most anyone had spoken to the girl since her father lay down one night and did not get up again. The gift of this stranger's focus made her hard seed of a heart soften. She opened her mouth to respond, but her mother was pushing her away, laying her own cheek over the place in her husband's chest where his breath clotted like spider's silk. Above the heads of her brothers Ilsa saw the stranger moving toward the bed. *To help,* she thought, and stood on her toes to see it.

Then her mother was wailing, her sons gathering around her or drifting from the room, according to their character. The stranger, too, had gone. Whatever he'd done to Ilsa's father, it hadn't saved him.

Now Ilsa was the daughter of a widow with six living sons. Her every minute was spent in the care of men, cleaning and feeding them, patching the holes they made in the world. Her eldest brother became master of the house, and power hung on him poorly. His natural indolence turned to outright sloth, his petulance to cruelty. His mother could not check him, and his brothers were badly influenced. Ilsa sought to survive by making herself invisible.

After a long hard year, the sickness that had taken her father came back. It moved through the village on velvet paws. Softly it padded into her own cottage, curling up one night on her eldest brother's pillow.

Ilsa knew she was a wicked, wicked girl. Because even as she sat beside him, wetting his slack tongue and wiping cool cloths over his face, she wished he would not wake. After a string of days and nights that melted together into one long twilight she walked into the sickroom to find the stranger beside her brother's bed. Two years had passed since her father's death, but she knew him at once.

His back was to her as he leaned over the sleeper. He did not turn before speaking.

"Go away, little girl who sees too much," he said in his voice like living stone. "Sleep without fear, the dream plague is passing. And I think your load will be lighter now."

Ilsa's mother cried out behind her. In the moment it took Ilsa to turn around and back again, the stranger had gone. Her brother's eyes were open, but they saw nothing.

Life was easier after he died. Without his cruelties to goad them, Ilsa's other brothers grew less crookedly.

Often she remembered what the stranger had said, and wondered if he'd had some hand in her brother's dying. Fiercely she told herself she'd thank him if she could.

Her chance came in summer, on a rare day when the sun shone so hotly even her village was warmed by it. Ilsa was twelve years old, carrying bread in a handkerchief and a skin of fresh milk, sneaking off into the trees. When she saw the far-off figure in a trim black coat, his hatless head and hands at his sides, she hurried toward him. Over the rutted path and into the trees, and no matter how she ran she could get no closer. Then she was in the woods, and could not see him.

"Ilsa."

The stranger spoke from behind her. He stood in the shadows just off the path, his face obscured and the rest of him carved into sunlit pieces.

"You see me still," he said. "I thought you might outgrow the habit."

She pressed a hand to her hammering heart. "I wish to thank you."

"For what?" he asked sharply.

Ilsa started to speak, but fear of her own wickedness stopped her tongue. Had this man really killed her brother? Could she truly be grateful to him if he had?

"I'm not accustomed to being thanked." His voice was gentler now. "Any more than I am to being spoken to."

"Why are you here?"

Though she could not see his face, she was certain he was smiling. The funny kind of smile people made when they thought a child was being foolish. "Do you pretend, still, not to know me? Those who see me once always do, and you have seen me three times now."

"Not your face," she ventured. "I've only seen your face once."

"And you'll see it again, in time. Here, come closer. Little daydreamer. Brave girl."

His praise poured over her bones like firelight. She moved toward him, straining all the while to see his face. The shadows over it held fast. When he reached out a hand her heart opened wide, but he did not touch her. He took the milk she held and poured it out, flinging away the empty skin.

"That is not for you. Not yet." And he slipped like a wild creature into the trees.

Ilsa walked home slowly, turning over the stranger's words and what he'd done. When she reached her yard, her mother ran to meet her.

"Did you drink it?" Her fingertips dug into her daughter's skin. "Did you drink the milk?"

Ilsa could only shake her head until her mother let go. The woman was weeping now, too hard to tell the tale, so one of Ilsa's brothers had to do it.

Their cow had been bitten by an adder with a slow-moving poison, he said, that bled into her milk but took hours to make her sicken. Ilsa's youngest brother had drunk straight from the bucket. Now beast and boy were dead.

Ilsa knelt beside his small body before it was buried, touching the peaks of his face beneath the winding sheet. She thought of the stranger in the woods and cursed herself for her foolishness. She knew, now, on what errand he'd come.

Had he held the boy's life in his pocket when he spoke to her in the trees? When he dashed the poisoned milk away, was it with the same hand that had closed her brother's eyes? Too long had she been foolish, but she would not be so now. If her burden was to see Death when he came, she would stop him before he stole from her again.

From that day forward, Ilsa carried a knife.

Ilsa was fourteen. She'd done her share of grieving, but so had everyone in her village. Death was not the courtly visitor she'd once believed him to be.

It was winter now, the woods blue and white and howling with a storm that seemed endless. Their stores were perilously low, their bellies churning. After three days of snow Ilsa's second brother ignored his mother's pleas and went out with his arrows and bow.

He did not come back. They slept and woke and slept again, and still he did not come back. His mother stood outside the door and Ilsa stood beside her, both glaring with streaming eyes into the snow. The longer they looked, the flatter it seemed, until Ilsa felt she could tear the world in two. Then she saw something coming, a dark lick against the white.

"There," she breathed, squeezing her mother's hand. "Right there. Do you see him?"

Her mother was silent a moment, peering where her daughter pointed. Then she turned away.

"There's nothing there. Come, you'll make yourself snowblind."

Ilsa did not follow her mother inside. Pulling her cloak more tightly around herself, she walked out to meet the figure in the snow.

He did not move as she approached. When she was still many yards distant, he held up a hand that stayed her where she stood.

"You killed my brother," she said. And though he was far away, she heard Death's voice as if he were right beside her.

"It is my nature to do so."

She'd hoped he might deny it. "He is dead then," she whispered. "How did it happen?"

His reply held no remorse, no pity. "Your brother was beguiled. After many hours wandering lost, the snow became alive to him. It broke apart into bright colors before him, and he became convinced he'd been delivered into a summer country. He took his clothes off and he froze."

Though Ilsa could not move to approach him, she could tighten her hand around her knife. "Come closer," she said. "I wish to say more to you."

"Do you think I can be killed? Do you think yourself the match of me?" There was curiosity in his voice, and a rough kind of wonder. It filled Ilsa's head like the buzz of honeybees. She closed her eyes.

"Do not court me," Death murmured from right beside her. She kept her eyes closed, knowing his nearness was an illusion. "Even I might yet be tempted. Do not court me before your time."

When she opened her eyes he was gone. She stood in the snow until her tears froze on her cheeks and she could no longer feel the cold, and still she did not turn toward home. What could she have to fear, when Death himself had left her alone in the storm?

Once Ilsa's mother had a husband and seven children. Now she was a widow with four. It was not so unusual in their village, where every family lived in Death's shadow.

Then one of her sons took his own life. Ilsa went to bed and he was living, she woke up and he was dead. She shook with rage at the cravenness of Death, who'd crept in and out when she was sleeping.

Three children left, and now the villagers shook their heads.

On a stinging autumn day one of Ilsa's brothers put his work aside and walked into the woods, where he scaled a tree to sit in its very crown, swaying with the breezes and laughing at Ilsa when she called to him. The wind kicked up and shook him to earth, and he died when he hit the ground. It happened so fast Death might almost have taken him in midair.

Two children now, and it hardened from rumor to understanding that the family was cursed. After that even the poor society of the other villagers was denied to them. Ilsa did not care—not yet. She was intent on meeting him again, that coward, Death.

Her last brother began to weaken. Not ill but grieving, staring for hours at the wall. He was afflicted with no sickness they could see; it must be his heart that had broken. When it became clear he'd die of it, Ilsa set her traps. Death was drawn to heartwood, it was said, so she whittled a piece of it into a hilt. Copper coins were used to weigh down the eyes of the dead; she smelted an old copper lamp into a new blade. She thought to draw Death toward her, and away from her brother.

What she would do when she caught him, she did not know. Sometimes the memory of his slow and ancient voice arrested her, and she fell into shameful daydreams. Sometimes rage at all he'd taken made her tongue and fingertips feel as sharp as her knife, and she believed herself capable of doing the impossible: of killing Death himself.

Ilsa's last brother slipped from her fingers and into Death's one very early morning. She'd left the room to fetch water. When she returned, she knew by the softness of his mouth that he was gone. The hearth was swept and the bedclothes straightened, as if Death had stayed a moment to tend to her work when his was done.

Ilsa prepared the body for burial, but without brothers to help her, the ground was too cold to dig. She laid her mother's last son over a pyre, and gathered bone pieces from the ashes to bury in spring. For days afterward, the scent of his burning clung to her hair.

Ilsa thought Death would come for her next, but he didn't. In a village whose houses broke their backs around growing families, too many mouths to feed behind every door, Ilsa was an only child, she and her mother two women alone. For that, they were punished.

The girl made a deal with Death to spare her, the villagers said. *She is his lover, his handmaiden, his helpmeet.* Even if she wasn't, the more pragmatic among them decided, she was at the very least a girl made for bad luck. Anyone could see it. And the village turned its backs.

Now Ilsa knew true loneliness. She felt too hollow to long for anything; revenge seemed as far from her grip as gladness. But she was not dead yet, and her heart not quite so hard as she wished it. The time came when longings returned to her. For company, for love. To speak to someone who wasn't her mother, whose mind now dwelled with the dead.

The village had as good as exiled Ilsa, but beauty speaks louder than banishment. She was seventeen when a young man came upon her daydreaming beneath a tree. She'd known him once, they'd played together as children. He hesitated a moment, then sat beside her.

Though they didn't speak much at first, he came back. By wordless agreement they met beneath the tree day after day. Soon Ilsa found herself taking joy in talking again, to someone whose own joy was mirrored back. The young man's name was Thom, and while she did not love him yet, she grew to love herself through his eyes.

Ilsa might have been content to keep Thom a secret, but after a year of clandestine meetings he asked her to marry him. He held her hand and looked at her tenderly, without seeing the battle within her. She did not wish to lose him; she did not wish to expose them both to judgment. She sensed, too, that she would always hold herself back from him, even if they were wed. There was a piece of her, buried deep as heartwood, that had already been claimed.

But she was so weary of being lonesome, so finished with silence. Beneath the tree that had shaded all their happy hours, she said yes.

That night Ilsa lay sleepless, her mind conjuring visions of married life from the dark. A big bed, a crackling hearth, a wooden cradle. The image of the cradle kept slipping away, warping into the shape of a coffin.

She sat up, sensing someone else with her in the dark. Not her mother, who slept in the next room, dreams weighed down with feverfew. The window was a gray mouth, the shadows beside it deeper than they'd been. A figure lingered inside them, the sight of whom made Ilsa's body melt like wax and spark like flame.

Are you here for me? She almost said it. Then the figure gave a sigh, soft as fur and touched with regret. The shadows shifted and lightened. She was alone again.

And Ilsa knew who Death had come for.

She ran to Thom's house in bare feet. She'd dusted her soles with her brother's ashes to remind Death of what he'd already taken. In her hand she held the fresh-killed body of a songbird Thom had given her. She wanted Death to scent her coming on the air. In her other hand she held her copper knife.

Thom's mother stood in their doorway holding a hatchet. She spat when she saw Ilsa.

"Get away from here," she said.

"A hatchet won't stop Death," Ilsa told her. "But I will. Let me in."

The woman looked her over, tangled hair and dirty feet and bird's blood dripping from her fingers. "It's true, then. You made a deal with Death."

"Death makes no deals, but he's made an enemy of me. Let me in."

Thom's mother let the hatchet fall from her shoulder. She stepped aside to let Ilsa pass.

The house was quiet. Death had already come for Thom's father, and marriage for his sisters. Thom lay in the center of the house's one room, hands full of earth to bind him. Bowls of moonlight on water lay at his head and feet to confuse Death. Ilsa knew he would melt through these snares like wet sugar.

She brushed the earth from Thom's hands with the hem of her skirt. She drank the moon-washed water. She dropped the songbird to the ground and crushed its bones with her ash-dusted foot.

When Death slipped in, he was smiling.

Ilsa thought she'd remembered his face, but she was wrong.

There were the pale eyes, the dark skin, the hair that wasn't any color she could place. The smile slow-growing and teeth hooked on lip and the broad hands almost lost in the unlit spaces of the cottage. But she'd forgotten the quickness in him, the sense of distance and open skies and hot sun and wide water, places she could only fathom the edges of. She forgot all the words she meant to say. Others took their place.

"Are you taking him because I love him?"

Death considered her. "You do not love him."

Ilsa's heart hadn't worked properly before. It learned only in that moment to beat. "Are you taking him because you love me?"

"I'm taking him because it is his time."

Her fingers squeezed and she remembered the knife in her hand. "I wish to kill you," she whispered. "For what you've done to me."

"Dying is the one journey I cannot take." Death held out a hand. "Now, girl who sees too much. Do you wish to know what it is I do, what it is I am? Take my hand, Ilsa, and stay a night with me."

She dropped her knife. Death's palm was hot and dry as dust, and when she touched him she could see a blood-bright door in the wall of Thom's cottage, where before there had been nothing.

"Open it," Death told her, and she did.

On the other side was a hallway of cool white stone. Ilsa forgot all she left behind the moment her cracked feet crossed over. She followed Death through passages filled with the sound of rushing water, up pillared stairs, to a room where a man lay on a black-draped bed, a crown in his wasted fingers. He was young, his eyes were bloodshot, and he was alone.

"Kings cannot escape me," Death said, and finally Ilsa saw what he did when he came to the dying. With long fingers he sieved the life from the king's mouth. It took the form of a steady blue flame, which Death tucked into the canteen that hung around his neck. He took Ilsa's hand again, and together they leapt through the window behind the king's bed.

They landed light as leaves in a night garden that smelled of lavender. An old woman lay among the flowers, an arm curled over her chest. The life Death pulled through her teeth was like a lock of bronze hair.

"The innocent cannot hide from me." There was a dark joy in his voice.

At the end of the garden was a pond. Ilsa followed Death into its waters. It swallowed them both, then spat them out onto the shore of a green island, lapped at by the Hinterland Sea.

A blue-eyed woman in traveling clothes stood at their arrival, drawing her sword. Death twitched his fingers like he was coaxing a cat, and the woman's life fled her throat. He seemed to marvel at it—a red wisp, like a twist of blown glass—before tucking it into his canteen.

"Those who hide cannot evade me," Death whispered, his breath crackling like cremation fire.

All night he led Ilsa from place to place, stealing

the life from men who cowered and women who wept, children who watched him through sickness's fog, and babies whose life-lights looked like glints of sun on water. Ilsa saw cobbled roads and the blood-dark sea. She saw valleys and clifftops. She saw palaces of ice and brick and marble and villages like her own, penned in by the trees. She walked with Death into a seaside cottage where a laboring woman grew pale, and through a throne room slick with the blood of a princess's fallen suitors. The hours passed and his head hung ever lower with the weight of his canteen.

When the sun threw its first light over Death's hands, he drew them back. He stood beside Ilsa in a cottage kitchen, where a man whose life was the color of a wren's feather lay dead over a soup pot. There was a door in the wall, a bloodred door Ilsa remembered walking through a lifetime ago.

She threw herself in front of it. "You cannot send me back."

Her night with Death had changed her, breath by breath. She couldn't go back to what she'd been. But the door turned to red smoke and he pushed her through it, back into the close air of Thom's cottage.

"I must," Death said. "But I'll give you a gift. For being my companion for a night, and in penance for all I've taken from you, you may keep this man's life. Do not fear, Ilsa. I will seek neither you nor him for many years."

Then he was gone, taking with him the scent of salt and wind, and Ilsa was alone.

Not quite alone. Behind her, Thom stirred. Around her, the village breathed, full of bodies that held a secret just behind the lips: a twist of colored light, faded or radiant as starshine, ready to be plucked by Death's fingers and tucked into his canteen.

Thom called her name, his voice warm with love. The room stank of broken fever. Ilsa turned until he could see her face outlined in the early light. When he spoke her name again it was a question, one she answered by walking from the cottage on dirty feet, caked with the mud, salt, and sand of the whole of the Hinterland.

After that night, the villagers changed their minds about Ilsa. *Miracle worker,* they called her. Weeks passed, then months, and Death did not return to the village. While Thom stayed away, the rest drew nearer. *Death's destroyer,* they said, and held her in reverence.

They could not know the new secret she held close: that she could see what curled behind their teeth when they spoke or laughed or whispered. Her night with Death had taught her how to spy the little lights the living carried in their mouths, and she could not unlearn the trick. She could read in the dull green flame that lapped between a woman's molars how she would live and how she would die. She could fathom a lifetime of lies and secrets in the snowy wisp circling a child's tongue. Between her own mother's lips she saw a life that had shriveled like a tree's last leaf, and must be taken soon. The only life she could not make out was her own.

This was Death's true gift. Not Thom's life, but Ilsa's

new vision, which carried with it a promise of madness. The little flames of the villagers' lives shimmered and coaxed, they showed themselves like red fruit. She understood Death better now. How could he deny himself such baubles?

But Ilsa would deny herself. She would not look, she would not see. Death couldn't stay clear of her forever. And while awaiting his return, and the reckoning that must come between them, she would pretend her life had not changed.

And so she did, until the day she looked up from trading whittled buttons for butter and found a baby watching her over its mother's shoulder. Its life was a tendril of soft metal singing over its gums. Ilsa knew exactly how it would feel on her fingertips if she took it, how it would rest in her palm.

In a cold haze she reached for it, fingers primed to pluck it free.

The child screamed and the mother turned, a knife already in her hand. She slashed at Ilsa's fingers, and Ilsa ran.

Her fury mounted as she went. Death had remade her. Did he truly think he would not answer for what she had become? She packed a blanket, her knife, and a waterskin, and left the village that had been her prison and her home. The whole wide world lay ahead of her, and Death hid somewhere in it. If he refused to return to her, she would go to him.

When darkness fell, Ilsa slept in her cloak by the side of the road. She would've died before morning if a twig hadn't cracked beneath the boot of the man leaning over her, his intentions clear in the jaundiced throb of his life-light. She opened her eyes and went for it without thought. It was a dull yellow over his tongue and came away easily in her fingers. The man's eyes went wide and stayed that way as he slumped over her in the leaves.

The light was heavy. She rolled it from hand to hand, remembering how Death had carried all the Hinterland's lost lives in his canteen. Into her drained waterskin she tipped the little light. Then she sat awake through the long night, knowing Death must come to claim it.

He never did. Was there no end to his cowardice? When the sun rose, she rolled up her blanket and kept walking. As she walked, she planned. Once she sought to make herself a lure for Death, and though he came, he did not stay. Now she would make herself something he could not ignore: a rival.

At first Ilsa tried to make sure they deserved it. She found low men who waited behind taverns with knives. Women who whipped their dogs and their children, merchants fat on coins who stepped on the backs of the lean to get more of them. The skin she carried around her neck grew heavy with lives, but never heavy enough to tempt Death.

She started to slip. She killed a man for speaking an unkind word to his wife, waiting until he slept to coax free the little light, then failing to resist the faint blue beat of his wife's. She wouldn't take the lives of children, she told herself, until she saw one with a dirty face that made her think of her youngest brother. The sight filled her with a hot, hard pain; in anger she peeled his light away.

If they'd lived, her brothers wouldn't have recognized her in her long black coat, her knuckles scabbed and her hair streaked with clay-white strands. Her own life was still the only one she couldn't see. If she could've she'd know it had been the color of sun through alder leaves once. Now it was the color of dirt dried hard on a dead man's boots.

Ilsa couldn't sleep the night she killed the boy who looked like her brother. Finally she drifted off with her back against the wall of a tavern. When she woke a man stood above her.

"No, no, no," he said, when she tensed to rise. "I've been watching you. I know what you can do, and I know why you do it. There's more I can give you than another bit of bait for your trap."

Ilsa looked him over, searching for his life-light, but his face was a scooped-out shell. She saw nothing in it. Ilsa hadn't been frightened in a long time. Not since she'd made herself the thing that was feared.

"Who are you, old man?"

"One like you, once," he said. "I sought to raise myself above my station. But I was cured of it."

"And? What was the cure?"

"This," he said, pressing something into her hand. "Drink it, and find the path you seek."

His smile was not a kind one. Ilsa was too hungry to notice. She looked at what he'd given her: a cut-glass vial the size of an acorn. Inside it swam liquid as thick as her hair.

Ilsa had seen the four corners of the Hinterland and the spaces between. She'd stolen the violet life-light of a despot prince, and descended a staircase into the sea, to walk among the gardens there. But she couldn't envision where the contents of the vial might take her. And if the old man was lying, and it was poison, well, she'd meet Death one way or another.

She tipped the vial to her mouth. Its liquid slid over her tongue and peeled back the skin of the living world, turning all its movement and color to shadows and smoke.

Among the shadows hovered a fine golden cord. It began just there, beside her hand. It felt alive as she wrapped her fingers around it and took one step, then another, following it hand over hand through the fog of the vanished world.

Her boots tumbled and turned over the unseen ground. After a time a pond appeared at her feet, glowing like quartz in the gloom. She followed the cord into the water until it closed over her head, and the mud disappeared from beneath her feet, and she dropped lightly into the land of the dead.

Death's realm was a silent one. She followed the shining cord through hematite forests, past lakes of frozen fire. She walked beneath the cut-crystal leaves of a grove of hazel trees, where misty figures spied on her from behind tourmaline trunks. Her heart beat faster to know she was close, that Death must soon receive her.

The waterskin around her neck sloshed with its burden of lives, growing heavier as she approached his castle.

It was an ugly place, a crouching animal bristling with spires. The cord led to its iron doors and ended at a ruby knocker. Shoulders aching with the weight of the waterskin, Ilsa heaved herself onto Death's doorstep. She knocked.

She waited.

An insubstantial figure opened the door and beckoned at her to enter. She followed it, boots echoing on the agate floors. She was led to a cavernous chamber whose ceiling was freckled with gemstones that glowed like stars. Music wound through the air like black flags, and the floor was full of slow-turning dancers. At the room's far end a figure sat easy on an onyx throne, eyes burning in his face like pale planets.

Death looked different in his own hall. He did not seem like a creature you could court or catch, or seek to make a rival. He looked at Ilsa and the music cut out, the dancers going still.

"Here I am," said Death. "Are you glad? You, who have sought me out and made made a mockery of the gift I gave you. Does it bring you joy to see my face again? Does it make you proud to look at theirs?"

The dancers turned toward Ilsa, and terror spread through her like wildfire. She recognized each one, because she'd killed them all. The man she'd slain her first night in the forest stood just there, holding a glass of something red to his lips. The child who looked like her brother sat on a table top, swinging his legs. Their faces were empty without their life-lights, their mouths filled with darkness. Ilsa took a step back, then fell to her knees, stricken by the weight of the lives she carried. With shaking fingers, she tugged at the strap of the waterskin.

It snapped. The skin tipped on its side as it fell, all the lights it carried spilling out. They spun over the floor and massed into a glittering fog that illuminated the faces of the dead before it swallowed them.

When the fog cleared away, the dead had changed. Their lights flickered from their faces, but what had been restored to them was only a kind of half-life. The sight of it stripped the blood from Ilsa's cheeks.

Death held up a hand, staying the crowd. "She is not yours to punish." He slid toward her and tipped her chin in his long fingers.

"The punishment must fit the crime. A theft for a theft."

The thing Death took from Ilsa wasn't her life-light. It was something that hid in her iris like a moon in eclipse and took the form of a fingertip-point of black glass. When it was gone she sensed a hardening come over her. She felt impervious, untouchable.

Death rolled the stolen thing over his palm. "This is your death," he said. "You wouldn't wait for it—you wouldn't wait for me—and so have lost your right to it." He popped it into a blank space between his molars for safekeeping.

"I promised you'd see my face again, and so you have. You will not see it again."

You may find Ilsa, if you seek her, sitting in a tavern or on a stone overlooking the sea. Following a plague wagon, lingering by the beds of the dying. If she looks back at you, you'll sense the hole in her, the nameless, missing something that makes you pull away. Her face will fade from your mind in time, until the moment of your own passing. And there she'll be, standing just behind Death's shoulder. Shake her off if she comes too near. Death won't let you into his kingdom if Ilsa walks beside you. Until his heart softens, she must make her long walk alone.

THE
SEA
CELLAR

At the edge of a great wood, on the shore of an inland sea, is a house where daughters go to die. But they go in lace and satin, with wedding rings on their fingers, so nobody dares complain.

In that house lives a man, some say. Others say a monster, and a few claim it's a woman who lives there, year after year, throwing out offers of good fortune to hook the desperate parents of unwed girls by the mouth.

And for every bride thus caught, traded for her weight in wealth or a business contract or a fleet of ships, there are those who come after her. The brides' secret sweethearts, grieving mothers, intrepid sisters and brothers prowl around the house at night, their footprints marking the sand, their horses breaking the branches. But none can find their way in without the house's leave. Though they can see the door right there, hung invitingly ajar, and the torches lit beside it, they could walk a day and night by torchlight and never get closer. It's on this threshold, weary and defeated, that the brides' lost loved ones stop, drop their sorrowful heads, and weep.

Sometimes over the sound of their own grieving they hear something else: a distant rush and fall, an endless shush as of one thousand men and women whispering. Not quite the water, not quite the woods, but something deeper, older. The voice, perhaps, that taught the sea to sing. Once this sound curls inside their ears, it will follow them to their final hour.

Alba was fourteen when her sister became a bride of the house. The dark dream of her sister's marriage began the night their father came home, as he often did, wet-lipped and stumbling. He pulled his eldest daughter from her bed by one soft arm and looked at her in the firelight. Her red hair and frightened eyes, the bloom of her hips.

"How old are you?" he said, and answered himself. "Old enough."

He'd wept then, molding his hands into a cup to hold her face. That was the most frightening thing to Alba, watching them from beneath the blankets. Their father was rarely cruel, but nor was he ever tender. He paid his daughters as much mind as he would a pair of barn cats.

"You were a pretty thing when you were born," he whispered, "hair red as a rose. Perhaps you'll be luckier than his other brides. At any rate, you'll be rich."

It wasn't until he slid a band of blue-green metal onto her finger that his daughters knew what he'd done. Everyone in that part of the world knew what the ring meant, whose suit it represented. Where it sat the girl's hand grew red with cold, then white. Try as she might, Alba could not warm her shivering sister. Nor could she remove the ring.

It took some listening at doors for Alba to learn the

whole sordid story of how her father traded her sister away.

He was sitting at the tavern in his usual spot, arguing over an unpaid bill, when a stranger approached. This man had yellow hair, the uncallused hands of a prince, and a blue silk top hat embroidered with sea nettles. He settled her father's account with a handful of gold. The two men then drank to each other's health, told tales, played dice, all without the other man revealing his name or his purpose. Over the sodden hours he prized from her father the long history of his failures, one confession after another.

Then he told him how he could make them go away. "It would be so easy," the stranger said, "to make you fortunate. You have two daughters, do you not? I need only one of them. Oh, no," and he laughed. "Not like that. I speak as a proxy for one who wishes to make your daughter a bride."

And he revealed on whose behalf he had come: the unseen resident of the house between the woods and the inland sea, which swallowed white-dressed girls and then sighed as if sorry for it.

How Alba's father must have paled! His blood run cold, his swimming head clarify. But the hook was already in him. How could he turn down good fortune, if all he must give for it was the hand of a daughter?

And maybe she would live. Brides went into that house, it was said, and did not come out. One each year and sometimes more, but it was possible that they *lived*.

That they were cherished and rewarded. A desperate father might imagine many hopeful things while wriggling on the hook. The ring was taken and the promise made.

The next morning a coach stopped in front of their house, dispensing a messenger bearing a long blue box. Alba watched from the window as the messenger, in hooded cape and gloves, knocked on the door. When she reached the front room, her mother was lifting a dress from the box. It was a shapeless thing of aged white silk, stained dark at the cuffs and smelling faintly of storms.

"You must stop this," Alba said. Fourteen years old and not yet hardened to the ways of the world.

"Who am I to stop what's already in motion?" Her mother spat on the floor. "I curse the one who sent this. I curse your father. As for your poor sister . . ." By then she was crying too hard to speak.

The messenger leaned against the wall, hands in his pockets. "What will happen to her?" Alba demanded. "Who is the bridegroom?"

"She has an hour," he replied. "I won't wait."

Alba found her sister in bed, beneath the blanket, and put her mouth close to the older girl's ear. "Run," she said. "To the woods. I'll gather what you need and follow after."

Her sister only sighed, and plucked at the ring, and turned her face away. Their mother stripped her down and tugged the dress over her head.

The family climbed into the carriage, silent as it carried them to a narrow house at a wooded crossroads where a judge answered their knock. They looked in dreadful anticipation for the bridegroom, but even the house's marrying was done by proxy. The one who took the groom's place wore a rippling water-blue coat and a mask that covered all but their lips. The bride shivered and wept and whispered her vows, holding tight to her mother when it was through.

Now, the proxy told them, the bride would travel alone, on horseback, to the house. She was allowed no belongings from her old life. She would wear the wedding dress and her hair combed down, left unpinned for the breezes to wind themselves through.

To her father, the proxy offered congratulations. "Go home," they said, "and see what fortune has delivered to you."

Alba watched with an aching heart as her sister was hefted onto a gray gelding. *Courage,* she thought, *take courage.* The weeping bride clung to the animal's mane, and their mother clung to Alba, and their father clung to the shrinking conviction that he had done the best a man in his situation could do. Alba fixed her eyes on her sister until she was too far gone to be seen.

When the family returned to their house, it had been transformed. Its two stories were four, its leaky walls snug brick, and every room was filled with riches and beautiful things. Her mother drifted through the house, tears drying. Her father seized up an overflowing coin purse and headed back out the door.

Alba walked the house's halls until she found the

room that was meant for her, full of books and candles and jewels and dresses, carpeted in the gray of her sister's gelding. She moved past these treasures, to the new looking-glass that hung on the wall. To her face in the glass, she made a promise.

She would not be so foolish as the other brides' sisters and sweethearts. She would not follow her sister uninvited, only to wander the woods and shore until the house's sighing drove her away. She would bide her time, plan and wait, and discover exactly what became of its brides.

Wealth was a balm to her mother's grief. Her father had no grief to remedy, and it did not take him long to imagine he'd earned the riches he traded a daughter for. The pair of them spent their days like they did the coins they hadn't worked for: without heed.

Across two long years Alba gathered whispers about the house that stood between the wood and the inland sea. She listened for tales of the brides it had taken before her sister, and for rumors of those who came after. Just two seasons after her sister's hasty wedding, a young woman from a nearby village was wed and fed to the house, following her father's loss of his fortune at sea. A year after that, the village cobbler abandoned his trade and set himself up in an opulent manor. He had a daughter of seventeen who had not been seen since before her father's sudden rise in life. Alba had a guess as to where she'd gone.

When Alba turned sixteen her mother began to

chatter of this eligible young man and that, without even the grace to blush over the subject of weddings. Alba, too, thought it time she marry, but her plans took a different shape.

She knew how it began. A man deep in his cups, heavy with desperation. A stranger's approach, and a bargain struck. Thus armed, she slipped from the house one night when she should have been sleeping. She walked to the tavern where her father had promised her sister away, and there watched for a man with yellow hair, smooth hands, and an embroidered blue top hat.

Many men came and went beneath her careful scrutiny. It was near dawn when she realized she was being watched, too, by a woman sitting in the farthest corner. Her hair was dark and her skin was rough, and her hat was blue silk and sea nettles. Alba looked back so boldly the woman laughed and moved to join her.

"Here you sit in this disreputable place, a lovely young woman, alone and"—she glanced at Alba's hand—"unwed. How did you fall so far?"

"I seek a husband," Alba said shamelessly. "I wish to marry a rich man with a big house, and no neighbors near enough to bother us. Do you know of such a bridegroom?"

The woman raised a brow. "You'll forgive me for not trusting a rabbit who lays its own head in the trap. What do you know of my business? What do you know of the house in the wood?"

Alba dropped all pretense. "Is it the house, then, that

the brides marry? Or is there truly a groom inside it? Is he a man or a monster?"

"Or a woman, some say." She looked Alba over. "It's not a husband you're seeking, is it? It's one of the brides. Your sister, was she? Your friend?"

"My sister."

"Steer clear of the whole dirty business, then. Your family does not need to sell two daughters."

"If it's such a bad business, why have a hand in it?"

The woman's mouth tightened. "Same reason as whoever sold your sister: I'm under a debt. Once I deliver a bride to the house, my debt will be settled. No one who works for the house does it for long, or knows any more than I do. If you wish to be the daughter who saves my neck, so be it. But I'll warn you once more. I believe the darkest things they say about that house are the truest. Let me feed to it a girl a bit more seasoned than you. Your courage can be turned toward better things."

Alba held out a hand. "I have waited two years to follow my sister, and answers are all I want for my dowry. If you're not the messenger who will deliver me, I'll wait for the next. But if you'd like to give your conscience a bride who went willingly, make your choice."

The woman drained her cup, then pulled from her inner pocket a ring that pearled with its own watery light. As the ring settled onto Alba's finger she felt a pressure like the grasping of a cold hand. In a moment she found she could bear the feeling. Her head steadied and she studied the ring, its dull marine gleam.

"May you discover the secrets you seek," the woman said. "May you make a joyful bride."

All that night Alba spun in the grip of strange visions. Of a house where blue light rippled on the walls and every room opened onto another in an endless twisting chain, and each bowl and basin clattered with wedding rings. She dreamed of orange and yellow creatures swimming through vaulted cathedrals, and woke with the taste of salt on her tongue.

At breakfast her mother's eye fell on Alba's new ring. She dropped her teacup to the floor, seized the girl's fingers, and wept.

After that it all happened quickly. The dress was delivered, stained and stinking, by a messenger who gave Alba an hour to prepare. On her sister's wedding day she'd watched as her mother did up the dress's long row of coral buttons. Now she had a lady's maid to do the work, with nervous fingers and a crooked hook. Once dressed she stepped alone into the waiting carriage, lit blue by the sun through its curtains. Waiting for her at the judge's chambers was another masked proxy, wrapped in a familiar coat.

Alba watched herself be wed from a distant place, lace scratching at her wrists and throat. The judge's voice traveled many leagues to reach her. At the end the proxy pressed their mouth to hers, lips warm with beeswax. Then she was lifted onto the back of a gray gelding.

Across two years she'd held fast to memories of her

sister, as the passage of time tried to steal them away. Now the lost girl seemed to ride behind her. Alba recalled her sister's kitchen scent of tea and thyme, the way she bit the knuckles of her right hand when she was nervous. Her habit of sleeping each night with a stitched fox on her pillow, left over from babyhood. If Alba never saw her again, she would always be the age she was when she left. Alba's age, sixteen.

Alba made herself one more promise. *The house will take nothing from me that I do not consent to give.* The trick, she knew, was to be ready to give everything.

Hair sweeping behind her, dress rucked up to her thighs, Alba rode.

She heard the house before she saw it. It did whisper, as the stories said. Or maybe it was the sea at its back that hissed and sighed. There were voices in the whispering that rose and fell, like the murmuring of a crowd gathered before a gallows. The house was a glow through the trees, then a shape rising between them, night birds wheeling over it like falling stars.

Mine, she thought. The ferocity of the feeling surprised her. But it was true, wasn't it? Even if she were to die tonight, she was married to the master or mistress or monster of this place. Right now, as she rode up to its gates, the house and all its mysteries were hers.

Her house was a grand place, white and silent. She admired its clean edges and the great golden eyes of its windows. Then she straightened her neck and rode on, fast through its open gates, pulling her horse to a halt in the empty yard.

She slid from the animal's back and led him to the stables beside the house, where a stall stood ready. When the horse had been tended to, Alba walked toward the inland sea.

It's breathing, she thought. Its waters moved up and down like the flank of a sleeping animal. *It would swallow me.*

Alba walked through the house's unlocked doors, into a vaulted hall. The whispering tugged at her ears, pieces of laughter caught in it like leaves in a river. A chair sat in front of a blazing fire, food and wine beside it on a silver tray. There was a card, too, marked with thin writing: *Please eat. Please drink.*

She tried to imagine her gentle sister reading these words, standing in this place, and having the courage to feed herself. Her sister had rarely gone farther than their yard if she could help it. But Alba had traveled a long way to trade her safety for a secret.

She sat. The food was hot, the wine was good, the fire stoked high. She drowsed in her chair, her head going hazy and the spitting of the fire rising up, becoming brighter, sweeter, until something woke her. She thought she'd heard singing through the floor.

The house's lights were turned down, blown out. Her tray had been taken away, the fire banked, and a lantern set on the table. Before she could reach for it, the lantern lifted into the air and bobbed off through the dark. Alba followed it up a long staircase, then another, and down a blue-carpeted hallway. The chamber the lantern led her to was lit by one hundred candles, vases of purple-throated flowers wobbling in their light. Before her lay the wide white stretch of her wedding bed.

Alba was brave. She was determined and she was sure and she had taken pains to make herself into someone who would not break like her mother, a woman of glass, or bend like her sister, a girl of wax. But she was sixteen years old, wed to a stranger who might have been a monster. When she lay down, she kept her boots on.

She waited. The candles burned low and the flowers withered in their heat. When the last flame had extinguished itself, the chamber door opened.

The tread across the floor was soft, so quiet she couldn't be certain anyone was there until their breath was in her ear: cool, smelling of salt and stone. It moved over her face and down to the neck of her nightdress. Then up again, breathing in her ear, breathing her in.

So this was the whim of the one she had married. Alba lay rigid, heart leaping, as a body lay down beside her. She felt the shifting of the bed and waited with crawling skin for the touch that must follow. Nothing happened, and nothing, and nothing. Her body ached from being held so still.

Then, a voice.

"What is your name?" it said.

She sat up, heart pounding with sudden fury. "Do you do not even know the names of the girls you wed? How many, now, have you taken into your bed? Do you eat them alive, or do you kill them first? What did you do with my sister?"

The pause that followed was so long she thought the voice wouldn't answer. Her heart was almost quiet again when it did.

"That's four questions," it said. "I will allow you just one each night. And for every question I answer, I'll take something in return."

"What will you—tell me what you will take."

"That depends on the question."

Alba thought a long while before she spoke again. "If I were to ask you, What has become of my sister?—what must I give you in return?"

"For that answer, I will take from you your shadow."

Alba tried and failed to imagine what it might mean to lose your shadow. "I agree to the trade," she said. "And ask you again: What has become of my sister?"

The voice replied without hesitation. "She came to me as so many of them do. Bewildered and weeping, expecting cruelty and finding none. I took from her what I take from all my brides: the things they do not need. With what was left I made something better."

Before she could protest this riddling response, Alba was struck dumb by a peeling, sliding sensation, a feeling like a carving knife being taken to all her edges. Not painful, but terrible all the same.

When it stopped she felt lighter, so awfully light, as

if her body might lift from the bed and dissipate into steam. Sleep swallowed her like the mouth of a fish.

When she woke there was a tray beside the bed with breakfast on it, and a ring of gold and silver keys. The keys were as long as her forearm and as small as her nail and every size in between. *The house is yours to explore,* said the note propped beside them. *But every room must be opened before you unlock the door that answers to the coral key.*

Among the hoard of metal keys was one the length of her thumb, made of bony orange coral. She looked at it closely before burying it among its kin. Then she set out to search for traces of her sister.

First she had to learn how to walk without her shadow. The air felt thin; she slid through it like an oiled blade. If she wasn't careful her body moved too fast, turned too sharp, stumbled. She was breathlessly, perilously light.

She opened the house's many doors. A key shaped like a musical note unlocked a room where the instruments played themselves. A key whose teeth had the smoothness of seeds led to a conservatory filled with trees in pots, bearing every kind of fruit. The tiniest keys opened minuscule doors, secret ones hidden in the walls, behind bookshelves, under vases. Behind them were rooms too small to crawl inside, every detail perfect, from the pages of books to the petals of flowers. Through the window of a room no wider than her palm, an unfamiliar moon poured its light over a sleeping city.

Behind a door whose key was as delicate as a fern

frond was a room full of marble statuary. Saints with fishtails, goddesses with serrated teeth, kings wearing whalebone crowns. In the room's center was a circular pool. Weightless as a wraith she stepped into it, shattering the statues' solemn reflected eyes. Water sluiced over her body like hands. When she put her head beneath its surface the whispering that filled the house's rooms sharpened into a wordless song. She listened to it, looking at a ceiling painted with the aftermath of a shipwreck: a vessel broken on rocks, men littering the water, women with fishtails taking them into their arms to kiss or kill.

As she opened each door, she pulled its key off the ring and left it in the keyhole. She looked at books she'd never heard of and ate from plates that never emptied, but found no trace of her sister or of the one who spoke to her in the night. When it was dark the bobbing lantern reappeared to lead her to a long dining table inlaid with abalone. Alba drank the wine, ate the bread, and returned to her chamber, wobbling with the heat of a hundred fresh candles.

She kicked off her boots and lay on the bed. When the last candle flame had drowned itself, the door opened. Again came the velvet tread across the floor. Again the briny breath running over her skin, no sound, no touch, and when it became too much to bear she lifted her own hand to feel for the one hovering over her. At once they drew back.

"Please," she said, desperate suddenly to see another living face. "May I look at you?"

The body settled beside her on the bed. "Is that your question?"

"No! I have another. If first you tell me what I'll lose if it's answered."

The speaker's pause was thoughtful. "Tonight I will take . . . your reflection."

Alba was silent. There was a time when she believed herself to be fearless, but there were trapdoors inside her, it seemed, beneath which fear could hide.

"Yes," she said, faintly. "You may have it."

The questions that had circled her mind all day seemed, in the voice's presence, like the bright thoughts of a sillier girl. "Tell me this," she said. "Who are you?"

"I am mother and murderer," the voice whispered. "I am womb and crypt. I am a road and I am the end of it."

No, Alba wanted to say. *No more riddles.* But the speaker took her reflection. It pulled free like a plant dangling roots, dragging little grief trails through her chest. With it went her memories of her own face, what she looked like smiling, sorrowing, what parts of it were like her sister's face, or her mother's. She had to run her hands over herself, her chest and belly and hips, to know she existed at all. The panic that came with the trade swept her under, and she slept.

In the morning she searched for her face in the breakfast tray and could not find it. She wondered what use the house could have for her shadow, her reflection. Perhaps there was a room where stolen pieces of the brides were kept.

All day she wandered. Through tiled rooms and

conservatories and a long, mirrored arcade. She could hear the singing clearly now. The song was everywhere, in every room, settling into her ears like foam. Words bobbed in it like boats; they were speaking to her, if only she could learn how to listen.

She had fewer keys left now than fingers. The last key, but for the one of coral, opened onto a kind of clue: a gallery whose walls were covered in painted women. Eyes light or dark, mouths sweet or cunning, faces full of mirth or sorrow or a secret. She might have seen her sister there, in a portrait whose eyes were dark and its lips unsmiling, but she couldn't be sure. In losing her reflection, she'd lost her sister's face, too.

In bed that night she waited impatiently. The candles burned down, they burned out. The tread came across the floor.

"Before you move any closer," she said, "tell me what I will trade away tonight."

The speaker in the dark took their time settling beside her. "Your voice."

"But—" Alba's heart struggled like a bird with honey-eyed wings. "How will I ask you anything after that?"

"You won't. Our game must come to an end tonight. Choose your final question with care."

And Alba asked a question she would soon answer for herself.

"What," she said, "is behind the door that opens with the coral key?"

The body beside her sighed in satisfaction. "Behind

that door is your true wedding bed. Behind it lies answers to all the questions you'll have no voice to ask."

Having answered, they took the thing they had
claimed.

Alba did not know her voice nestled in her chest like
a ripe peach until it was taken from her. She did not understand the joy of taking bites from that endless peach
every time she uttered a sound. But when it was gone
she felt its absence, perfectly round and aching like an
empty stomach.

This time, the plundered bride did not allow sleep
to take her. She stood, picking up the ring from which
the coral key hung, and went in search of its master.
She passed ironbound doors and doors of soft wood,
doors with keyholes where they ought to be and ones
that were hidden, disguised as the leering eye of a
satyr or the open mouth of a witch. She followed the
sound of singing downward, to a slanting cellar door
in the house's very depths. Behind it the singing rose
higher, keening and victorious. She could hear the
words now.

The bride slid the final key into its lock.

When she opened the door the light that poured
through was blue and silver and green and white. It was
black and red and every color she could put a name
to. Her bridegroom stretched before her, its breath on
every part of her. She would call it by its name if she
could speak it: *the Sea*. All the brides were waiting, eyes
brimming, hands outstretched, legs fused into shining
fishtails. One had a face very like her own. She was as

light as them now, her heart as eager. Without reflection or shadow or voice, she moved toward their reaching arms, their braided siren song. She knew another voice would be fashioned for her soon, some absolute piece of her flayed into a thing that crackled and keened. That lured and crawled.

The door shut fast behind her.

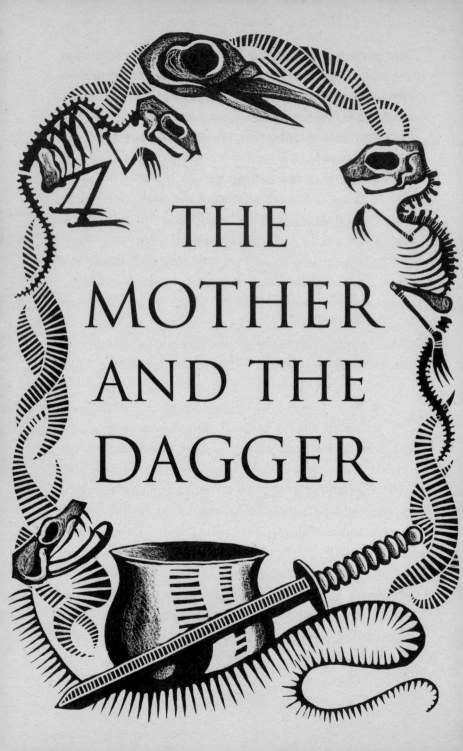

THE
MOTHER
AND THE
DAGGER

Wherever you live, there are rules you must go by.

Tales are told of a village so plagued by ghosts that bells are hung over the doors, to keep them from slipping in at night. In certain houses the cooks bake three loaves of bread, two to eat and one to bury. In some towns you would as soon slit your own throat as wear red in winter or yellow on a wedding day. And even kings must bow low when they see a dead man walking, lest the departed take offense, and take hold of their hand.

In this place, a village so small a child could stand at one end and toss a stone to the other, there is one rule: you must never sleep beside an open window.

But it's hot. Torturously so. Hotter than your own breath, the air so ripe and still you could prick it with a pin. And such rules are faded things, softened by time.

Rise from your bed now, and walk to the window. Put your hand to the glass and push it, just enough to let the night air in. Listen to the sounds of the woods after sundown. Sliding leaves and courting crickets and all the guileless creeping of the creatures who make their homes in the dark.

There's something else out there, too. Open the window wider to hear it. From beneath the whispering trees comes a singing, not of one voice but many, lifting in a silvery lament.

Look back toward the safety of your bed, just once. Then lift yourself up and out the window.

Walk down a path picked out for you by the helpful moon, then leave it. Let the voices sing you all the way to a little house hung with wind chimes, painted gray by the shadows of the overhanging trees. The chimes, you realize, are what you've been listening for. From each rings a human voice.

Step closer and see what they're made of. Bones, curving and fine, drifting in a breeze you can't feel.

Step closer still. Hear the singing refine itself, becoming a single voice that speaks to you alone. Walk nearer once more and tilt your head close. These bones wish to tell you a tale.

You are far from your bed, they begin. *The night is young now, but getting older. Listen while you can, to the story of how we came to be what we are. It begins with the tale of a princess, and the longing that undid her. Of how she became the Mother, and turned her dagger toward terrible things.*

First there was a king (so whisper the bones), and the princess who bewitched him. Their kingdoms adjoined each other, but a great wall of thorns and roses grew up between them. The wall had been raised by a sorceress of the princess's kingdom, where magic was commonplace, to divide it from the king's, where magic was reviled.

By rights the two should never have met. But the summer the princess was eighteen, the heat grew so fearsome the roses fell like lopped heads, and the thorns and all their vines withered to dust, and for the first time in a dozen ages the way between kingdoms was clear. As a gesture of peace the unmagical king visited the princess's father. When he and the princess saw each other, they fell deeply in love.

Though her parents and his advisors tried to put them off the match, they would not listen. The night before their marriage the king extracted a promise from his bride: that, from the moment they were wed, she would forsake magic completely. The princess vowed to obey him in this, and their hands were joined.

For many months the king and his new queen were happy. But one thing stood in the way of perfect contentment: a year passed, and then another, and the pair remained childless.

Softly, the queen's thoughts turned to the uses of magic. Harmless things at first. Herbs, swallowed beneath the swollen moon. Incantations, burnt buds, small offerings. Nothing worth troubling the king. But when the hearth magic of which she was capable did nothing, the queen grew desperate.

In her father's kingdom, friendly to enchantments, deeper magic could be worked. And the queen made her plans.

"I dreamed last night that my father lay ill," she told her husband. "I must go to him at once."

The king was uneasy. Prophetic dreams shifted too close to the tricky terrain of magic. But he trusted his wife, so he kissed her and let her go. After a few days' travel, she and her retinue reached the borders of her father's kingdom. Though they could have made the palace by nightfall, the queen ordered her people to make camp, fed them the wine she had drugged for this purpose, and rode out alone once the last of them was sleeping.

She rode not to the palace but to the cottage at the edge of it, where the royal sorceress lived. The woman had foreseen her coming, and knew the wish that lay in her heart. The sorceress's own heart was hardened toward the queen, who, having forsaken the magic she was born to, now crept back to it in the dark.

Nevertheless she received her royal guest with deep genuflections and crocodile tears. "I am honored," she said, "and I know what you wish of me. But I beg you to think again. The cost will be too much."

"Save your weeping," the queen said, knowing the woman despised her. "I care no more than you what your magic may cost me. I must have a child."

Dry-eyed, the witch sat up and studied the queen. There were things she could do for her. And though it was true the cost of any action would be great, some costs were greater than others. She chose her next words as carefully as an executioner selecting her blade.

"Yes," the witch said softly. "I will save my tears, and weep for you once you've heard what I ask for." She took from a chest a little knife, its enameled handle set with red apples, and a glimmering metal bowl.

"Tomorrow night, when the moon is high, you will

take this dagger and cut out your tongue. Collect the organ and all its blood inside this silver basin, then bring it to me. I'll simmer the thing by moonlight, over a peat fire, and you'll eat it from root to tip. Once that has been done, the signs of pregnancy will come quickly. By season's turning, you'll have your child."

The queen looked at the witch a while in silence, considering her price. The violence of it, of her own hand being set to it. But she could do it, she thought. So long as she did not lose her grip.

"Yes," she told the witch. "I will."

Under advancing dawn she rode back to her retinue, lay as if sleeping among them, and waited for their drowsy awakening. The party rode on to her parents' palace, where they were received with celebration. She pretended relief at her father's being well, and spent the day visiting with her mother and sisters. When the palace was asleep she took the witch's dagger and basin into her father's courtyard and made ready to cut out her tongue.

She tried, and tried again. But her hand and her nerve failed her. Finally, weeping at her own cowardice, she lit on a deception. From an old dress she cut a length of red velvet. The cloth grew lively as she cut, writhing under the bite of the witch's enchanted dagger. The queen stuffed it with sawdust and sewed it into the shape of a tongue. Then she slashed the inside of her elbow and let her blood fall into the basin until the velvet tongue was soaked through.

It was only her blood the witch truly needed, she told herself. The old woman meant to make a fool of the queen.

Mouth shut tight, she delivered to the witch the bloody basin. The old woman did as she had promised, cooking the false organ over a fragrant fire. Quickly the queen swallowed it down, eager for the whole business to be finished.

At once she felt a thump in her belly, as of something dropped with force. She pressed a hand to the place and smiled with closed lips.

The witch smiled, too. "Good fortune to you, highness. May you get the child you paid for."

For a time the queen did not open her mouth but when she was alone. She did not speak or sing or eat in company, or part her lips beneath her husband's. She dared not risk the witch hearing of her treachery.

But as her stomach ripened, she forgot to be cautious. She had paid for her baby in blood; why pay a second time in silence? Now she spoke and drank watered wine and spent long hours with the king imagining their child's bright future. The queen was always happy in those days, though sometimes she thought it unusual the way her baby moved in her. Other women spoke of their children kicking and swimming and turning about. Hers seemed instead to twitch, to wetly slither.

She did not linger too long over these thoughts. Already she loved her child fiercely.

Her time came, and the king paced outside the door. All went as it should until the queen began to push.

The baby's hands came first, reaching blindly from her womb. Beneath the midwife's watering eyes, it pulled its body after.

The queen wore rings on every finger. Jewels winked from her ears and throat. When she saw the nature of the thing she had birthed, she stripped her hands, her neck, her earlobes and wrists. She split the riches between the ashen midwife and her assistant. Knowing that might not be enough, she whispered promises of what would become of them if they spoke a word about what they'd seen. Of the dreadful things she, a queen raised in a kingdom of magic, could do.

That done, the queen held her baby close. It was long and thin, its sawdust weight lopsided in her hands. Its eyes were wood-knot whorls, oddly alert, and its skin was velvet. She began to nurse it, not at her breast, but on blood from her bitten tongue. As the creature lapped up the stuff, its skin grew fleshlike, its gaze almost indistinguishable from a real child's.

The queen knew enough of magic to know the effect would fade. The child must be fed regularly, and in secret. She would gladly give every drop of blood in her body to keep it safe and close. It was her only child.

She bade the midwife open the door, so the king might meet his son.

The queen was slow to recover. With his own hands her husband fed her bone broths and bloody cuts of meat, candied nuts and the furred halves of peaches. Still she was wan and weak, crooning over her baby, tucked in bed with it at all hours. The king had the sense, half-formed, that the child was to blame for her somnolence: his wife would not hear of separating from it for any length of time.

But she could not refuse her husband when he begged her to try, at least, to leave her bed. To put the baby in its cradle and lean on his arm. Dizzily she stood. No sooner was she upright than she swayed and stumbled, and fell to the ground.

When the queen regained her senses, she was tucked in bed. Her child was no longer in the room.

"It's for your own good," the king said soothingly. "Our son is strong, he weakens you. He'll have a wet nurse until you're well again."

An hour later, the king's blood still red beneath her nails, the queen lay in a poppy-induced sleep. Her husband walked through the palace unseeing, his wife's screams echoing in his ears. The red tunnels her fingers had dug glistened freshly over his cheeks.

She was sunk beyond screaming now, but some-where, across the palace, another voice cried out. That of a nursemaid who'd peered at the child in its cradle.

Without the queen's blood, her baby's eyes lost their living shine. While she slept, the grain of its skin soft-ened back to velvet. The thing the king called *son* was now just as it had been when it dragged itself from the queen's womb: a velvet poppet with wooden eyes, stuffed with sawdust. His horror of the thing was more vicious for having curdled from love.

When the queen woke in a cold room, her husband was beside her. Though he heard the change in her breath, from sleeping to awake to afraid, he did not lift his head.

"What punishment would you recommend," he said at last, "for a wife who deceives her husband? Who defies and deceives and defiles. Whose dark arts stain his person and his crown and that which he cherishes most. What punishment has such a woman earned?"

Her child was dead, or whatever passed for dead when applied to a thing that was never truly living. The queen could feel that it was gone, undone, its small strange place in the world scratched out. In a voice that was pitiless, she answered her husband.

"You must take a barrel and drive one hundred nails through it. The wife must be stripped naked and placed inside the barrel, and its lid pounded tight. The barrel should then be rolled through the kingdom with the wife inside it, to the place where a bonfire waits to swallow her."

The king did not seem to hear her.

"Banishment," he said. "That will be her punishment."

The queen who was no longer a queen was delivered to the end of her husband's kingdom, where a wall of thorns and roses once grew. There they left her, a single man staying behind to make sure she didn't reenter the kingdom. He watched as she walked away from the road that led to her parents' palace, into the wild woods that belonged to no king. He kept his eyes on her back until she was lost among them.

The queen, whom we must now call the Mother, still had the witch's apple-handled dagger. She knew from cutting the velvet that made the false tongue, that made the false child, that the dagger had some measure of life-giving properties. She comforted herself through her days of grief and exile by using it to make all manner of things into children: cut flowers that spun their petals at her after she sliced through their stems, wood carved into babyish shapes that wriggled over her hands. As she had done with her child, she could make the life in these objects last longer by feeding them on her blood, but always their capering turned at last to stillness.

Some months after her banishment, the Mother sat in solitude in the crude shelter she'd built herself, whittling and weeping and singing a cradle song. She heard something shuffling through the trees and waited to see what might present itself. *Death,* her heart whispered, a prayer of longing.

It was two children who broke at last from the woods, their faces filthy and striped with tears. Brothers, abandoned by their own parents, they'd heard the Mother singing and drew too close.

She dropped her dagger and held out her hands.

Mother took them in. The boys built for her a new shelter, a sturdy, beautiful cottage. They taught her things a queen doesn't know. Which plants to eat, where to set your traps, how to boil hickory root into salt. She sang to them and told them tales of kings and queens, and at night she kissed their cheeks and locked their door against the dark. The three lived happily for a time, until the night came when her sons discussed their plans.

"I'd like to have a farm one day," the older boy said. "As our father did before he lost it."

Mother was whittling with her little dagger; now her hands went still. "Would you go so far from the woods?" she said faintly.

"I wish to go even farther," said the younger boy, stoutly. "I wish to spend my life at sea."

She listened to them, knuckles whitening around the handle of her dagger. The firelight painted their faces with unfamiliar shadows, and they seemed suddenly to be strangers.

No, she decided. They would not leave her. They would not go away. It wouldn't do for her to lose her children.

All the next day she doted on her sons, holding them close and feeding them good things, laying her hands on them whenever they were near. Despite the sweetness of her attentions the boys were uneasy. They shifted and slunk like animals before a storm, and couldn't put a name to their fears.

When the sun went down she bade them lie with their heads in her lap. They looked swiftly at each other, but still they did it, their hair tangling over her knees as she sang the lullaby that once lured them from the woods. When their eyes fell shut she kissed them on their temples and mouths. They could taste her intentions in the salt of her tears, but it was too late. With her dagger, made of magic and sharper than most, she severed their heads from their necks.

As quickly as their own life left them, their bodies were animated by the borrowed life of the magic dagger. It made their viscera unpack itself, it made their bones lament and sing. And the Mother's heart sang with them, because she saw she had been right. Her children would not leave her now, they would always be with her. She strung their bones into windchimes that filled her little clearing with the music of their wistful voices.

So it went. There are always lost children, and woods to hide them, and the Mother waiting in her cottage with a smile on her lips. And if rumors of her reach the villages that grow beyond the trees, they are told in twisted whispers.

There's a woman in the woods who longs for children. There's a house hung with singing bones. Do not sleep with your window open at night, lest they sing you away from home.

The bones fall silent. You stand alone in the darkest part of the night. Far behind you is your room, your bed, your life, all so distant they might as well be dreams.

The door to the cottage is opening now, letting out sweet smells and firelight and a woman so beautiful you forget the bones' tale. Her white dress, her black hair. Her smile so soft and inviting. A mother's smile.

She runs a hand over her bone chimes to make them sing, and reaches the other out to you.

"Won't you come closer?" says the Mother. "Won't you come in?" And you do.

TWICE-
KILLED
KATHERINE

An enchanter lived in a house with rooms beyond counting, in the shadow of an ancient oak. He had a string of wives behind him and as many children as his house had doors, because when he was young he'd learned the secret of long life. Using sweet smoke and words stolen from a witch, he'd coaxed his own death from his body, hidden it in an acorn, and buried the acorn below his window. The branches of the oak that rose from the acorn still tapped against the glass, but the wise old face in the tree's trunk that once spoke to him had long ago gone quiet.

The enchanter, rich and as handsome as he'd been when he seduced the witch who gave up the words, had no shortage of wives when he wanted them. His latest was beautiful and young and prouder than he'd given her credit for, with a will nearly as strong as his own. She was determined he would end his dalliances with the servants and in town, and fixed her heart on making his life a misery if he didn't. And so, when the stable master's wife told the enchanter she was carrying his child, he was set on keeping it a secret.

After receiving word that the midwife had come to the stable master's cottage, the enchanter dispatched the raven that was his familiar to stand watch at the window. The laboring woman saw the black bird peering in and was afraid, for herself and the child she carried.

When the baby came it was red-haired and blue-eyed, with a hard chin and blade-cut mouth, every inch the enchanter's child. But the stable master's hair was ruddy enough, and a purse of gold convinced him to accept the girl as his own.

She was called Katherine, and she grew up in solitude. Her mother resented being closeted with a baby in their crude quarters, and the stable master didn't care for children. Katherine would have been lonely had she not learned, early on, that she had a powerful affinity for growing things. She gave flowers new ambitions, convincing them to creep free of their beds and up around her windowsill. She coaxed a bounty from her mother's mean kitchen garden and made the grass around their door grow thick and high, never suspecting she was drawing from the slipstream of magic that ran in her blood.

But she was always fascinated by the enchanter's oak tree. His servants knew without being told that the oak was not to be disturbed, never pruned nor otherwise tended. Even its shade was shunned, having an unsettling texture to it, that of something you could peel back and fold or step into and be lost completely.

Katherine did not share their fears. When she was old enough to crawl, she crawled toward the tree. When she learned to run, she ran to it. Her miserable mother always caught her, until Katherine grew old enough to care for herself and her mother gave up trying.

"Go," she said, "and curse yourself if you wish. Let the old tree swallow you, or the ground, for all I care. Let the enchanter himself find you and beat you, if it teaches you at last to be still."

Katherine took her mother's abuse in silence, as she always did, waited till the woman wasn't looking, and fled to the tree. Over the creek, past the stables, through the enchanter's gardens, to where its shadow spread over the grass like a pool of black water. It was cool and dark and slightly binding, clinging to her skin. She laid a hand on its bark and felt it grow keen beneath her fingers. It was the same feeling she had when making a tomato plant grow out of season, or convincing a bush that bore only leaves to bud with flowers.

She put a foot on the trunk and settled her fingers in its furrows. She began to climb.

Though the enchanter's body was young, his mind was old beyond reckoning. He looked sometimes at the age-twisted oak and marveled that he'd known it when it was a dream inside an acorn. His mind still ran like quicksilver, still sparked like water over rocks in sun, still wondered and lusted and questioned and raged, but sometimes when he looked at the tree's scarred trunk he felt very old indeed.

It was one such time when—as he gazed into its shifting leaves—the enchanter saw another face peeping out at him. It was sharp and fearless and a cunning kind of quiet. It looked just like his own. Having long forgotten about the stable master's wife and his little red-haired by-blow, the enchanter was startled, a thing he very rarely was.

"Who are you?" he asked, in a voice that sounded less than commanding. "Are you my death returned?"

The creature in the tree said nothing.

"Do you come to remind me of my own mortality?" he said. "Go back, feed the oak, and be patient. I have much work to do before I have need of you."

Katherine watched him in startled silence, and he might have turned away still believing her to be his long-deferred death, having crept up out of the acorn to glare at him. But just then she lost her footing. As she clung to the branches, her face colored with surprise, and he realized she was quite human. A child. And he remembered the baby who had looked at him with such composure more than a decade ago, when he went to strike a deal with the cuckolded stable master. In one motion, he lunged over the windowsill—his body stretching unnaturally, arms long as branches—and pulled the girl into his house.

Katherine knew when to be quiet. She knew how to stand very still, so she no more caught the eye than a footstool did, and if she were to be kicked or slapped, it would be with the impersonal violence enacted upon an inanimate thing.

She stood before the enchanter, in his rough brown robe with its sleeves pushed up and the raven on his shoulder. His face was so exactly like her own that it answered a question she'd never thought to ask.

"Are you not afraid of my tree?"

His voice was stern, but she sensed he was pleased by the notion. She shook her head.

"They say the touch of its shade will flatten you like a flower and deliver you straight to Death. They say the nod of my head could flay you where you stand, that my voice alone is deadlier than a goblin's kiss. Are you unafraid, or just foolish? Do you not believe what they say about me?"

Katherine's face was composed, but he saw the nervous motions of her fingers. Then he saw what was happening beneath them: flowers, growing from a crack in his windowsill. They budded and bloomed and died and began again. She spoke no words, looked only at him, but under her hand there was magic.

When his children came of age, the enchanter would test them to see if they'd inherited his abilities. On finding them lacking, he sent them out into the world, to marry or seek their fortune or do whatever they wished, so long as they never returned to his house. Katherine was the first of his offspring to have his gift, and he meant to teach her.

That first day he didn't let on to her that he saw what she was doing, and that its name was magic. Instead he let his oak lean close to the window, so she could go out the way she had come. He meant to prepare his workshop for a student, who would, in time, become an enchanter herself, one he could hold in his thrall and use as a secondary source of power. It was lucky she was a woman, and simpler to sap.

When his preparations were made he sent a servant to fetch her, and learned she could not come. The wasting sickness that paced the nearby town had reached the stable master's house, and Katherine had fallen ill. He worked out how to save her, brewed a tincture that could do it, but when he carried the medicine to her cottage she was already dead.

The enchanter stood at her bedside, looking upon the withered little face so much like his own. Her mother gaped at him, dry-eyed and very far from the fox-pretty maid he'd once sported with in the rooms of his house. Something moved in him, a weakness he hadn't faced since divorcing himself from death: grief. For just one moment, he mourned the dead girl in the bed. And before he could think better of it, his hands were weaving the air, turning it thin and bright and unbreathable, as he worked a heavy enchantment. It made his bones creak and brought out lines of silver in his hair. It made his oak tree drop its leaves and groan low, the sound of it running through his house and filling its occupants with dread.

He could not return the girl's life to her: it was gone. He could not take her death away: she'd already spent it. So he gave her a different kind of gift. Her body was freshly dead, still warm. And where there's warmth, there is hunger.

He gave that hunger eyes. He gave it will. He

shaped its formless turning into something pointed as a dagger. That dagger cast about the room, seeking the life it longed for. Drawn in by the beat of blood and breath and the high curdling flavor of fear, it fixed itself on Katherine's mother, fitting its invisible mouth to hers and drawing out her life. As the woman's hair faded to ash and her bones curled in like fingernails, the girl on the bed shifted. She moaned. She opened her eyes.

Katherine was not unchanged by death.

When her body uncaged her mind, it went far below. She found herself in Death's kingdom, that airless realm of mineral trees and floors of blue agate, where there is no sun or sky, but a distant pearly ceiling.

She reached for her magic, that green-fingered ability she drew on without knowing its name. In a land where nothing grew, she couldn't find it. She wanted to panic or grieve, and could discover the capacity for neither. Death's kingdom was no place for rosebuds or high emotions. Katherine felt herself shrinking in its fist, felt the shearing of her power and the ebbing of her fear, when suddenly she was blinking, breathing, crying out on her own hard bed, in her own ravaged body. Life buzzed inside her like a fly seeking escape, throwing itself at her borders.

She didn't know the life was her mother's. The enchanter told her nothing about it. But she was never easy with that life inside her. It was a flame too long given to flickering. And while she forgot her hour in the land of Death, it had left its mark on her. Her bright hair now ran black. The gardens she tended grew florid with red flowers and dark fruit that numbed the tongue and drugged the senses. All the fresh green things she tried to grow collapsed into rot.

Katherine was not the only victim of the wasting sickness. The enchanter's own wife walked into Death's kingdom three days after Katherine left it. With no woman left to appease, the enchanter brought his illegitimate daughter to live inside his house.

Her power grew by the day. She could make things move outside of their natures, she lit candles with a snap. She made her father's eyes ignite with a radiant greed, though at first she saw only the radiance. Dreamier than she'd been before dying, she was still quick-minded, clever, and keen to learn.

Katherine grew up in pieces. Her limbs then her face then the rest of her, until all at once she was a woman, legs too long beneath the hems of her dresses and hair still braided back like a girl's, framing the fine gull curves of her bones. Proud not only of her skill but her beauty, the enchanter had a new wardrobe made for his daughter and hired a maid to keep her. And on a spring day so fresh and soft and wet it seemed it could break apart in your hands, he packed her into his fine carriage to show her off to the only one in the world whom he counted as his equal.

The man they were visiting was another enchanter who'd deferred his death. Though the two old foes despised each other, they gilded their envy and scorn with fine words, meeting every ten years to exchange gossip and brags. While the other enchanter traveled widely and took many protégés, Katherine's father lived his lifetimes in one place, and had never before had a student worth teaching. He wished to show his friend and enemy that he had sired a true enchanter.

On the day they rode out, a week of heavy rains had sent the river welling past its shores, turning the road into a ribbon. The water carried in its arms not just fishes and fallen leaves but ladies' shoes and gemstone buttons, polished bones still sighing, a cradle and a wooden doll with no mouth, a dead rivermaid wrapped in weeds. Katherine gazed into the waters, dreaming. When they arrived at the other enchanter's house, in a prosperous town on the banks of the river, she felt as out of place as the mouthless doll.

The other enchanter's face was even younger than her father's, frozen forever at twenty. He had yellow hair and eyes as old and cold as the stars. When he laid them on Katherine their force was such that she startled, a poppy blooming in her right hand and a black plum in her left.

The beautiful man took her plum and bit into it, letting its juice run into the golden hairs of his arm. He licked it off and smiled at her.

Katherine took pains not to be alone with her father's rival. His eyes followed her about the room, sliding over her skin like willow whips as he watched what she could do, in the exhibitions of ability her father insisted she perform. They were to stay with this enchanter for a week, long enough for the two men to deride old acquaintances, exhaust their boasts, and finally grow so disgusted with each other they couldn't bear to meet for another ten years.

Four days had passed when the golden-haired enchanter let himself into Katherine's room. It was late, but she heard his key in the lock she'd so carefully thrown, and was sitting up in bed when he opened the door.

"What will you do?" he asked playfully, when he saw her expression. "Throw plums at me?"

She did. She brought all her magic to bear on confounding his path between the door and the bed. But she was young, and he was ancient, and her power to his was as a drinking cup to the sea. Or so he thought, and she believed.

He reached her, still laughing, his skin glowing in the candlelight. The feeling of his magic overpowering hers was a press at her temples, a cold absence in her hands. When he seized the front of her nightdress, she abandoned magic and went after him like a cat fighting its way from a sack. Her nails found his cheeks, her teeth his throat, her knee the place between his legs. With a curse he rendered her still as the dead, nothing moving but her eyes and her tears and her drumming heart.

No violation was enough for the wound she'd dealt his towering pride. He took his knife from his loosened belt and ran it down the side of Katherine's face as steady as a finger, watching her eyes widen in agony. Maybe it was the pain that allowed her to move just for a moment, long enough to lift her head and spit in his face.

When her spittle hit his cheek, his mind was turned from thoughts of lust. He stopped caring whose daughter she was, and what the cost might be if he broke her. He pressed his thumbs to her neck, slippery with blood, and squeezed.

"In my own house," he hissed. "You bastard girl, you witch, you vile thing."

Katherine's vision ran with bubbles like black Champagne. She heard a voice in her ear, low and triumphant. *I have you,* Death said. *I have you again.*

Then the dark wrapped her up completely and she stood once more in that silent underground land that smelled like nothing and glittered with precious ore. The place where her stolen life had lodged was empty again, gaping like a throat and made willful by magic. As Katherine looked about herself below, her hungry body stole the life from the golden-haired enchanter above.

So intent was he on killing her, only death could loosen his hands from her neck. She woke soaked through with blood from her wounded face. The enchanter's body lay cooling on the floor.

It was luck that made her father find them before the servants did. The man was not entirely insensible to his old foe's attentions to his daughter, and came too late to look in on her. When he saw the other enchanter dead and Katherine alive beside him, he paused for just a moment, his face showing more cunning than regret. Swiftly he packed their belongings, and a number of the other man's treasures besides. Before the sun had risen, they were on the road toward home.

If Katherine's first death left its film on her skin, her second dragged behind her like a mantle. Her footsteps made no sound, as if she walked again in the noiseless realm she remembered only in sleep. Her black hair blazed with a sharp white stripe.

Her face healed poorly, the scar left by her attacker's knife clotting at her chin like candle wax. The enchanter could have healed it, but a scar was no barrier to magic, so it didn't occur to him. Katherine might have removed it herself, but chose instead to grow accustomed to her altered reflection.

More than that had changed. While her father treated her as he always did, she saw different things in him now. When he smiled, she sensed his hunger. When he touched her, rarely—a tap on the hand, fingertips on her shoulder—she felt the faint buzz in it, not of love or affection but something darker, deeper in the bone. She could hardly bear his nearness.

Twice dead now, Katherine knew herself to be a thing that blocked the light. When her father took her to town, conversations cut out and laughter went cold. The townspeople feared the ageless enchanter and his heavy raven and his unspeaking mirror, the daughter who walked at his side. Her shadow had something of the oak tree's about it, a depth and weight that made the unmagical shrink away.

She wondered, still, about the oak tree. She'd never forgotten the words the enchanter had said to her as she perched like a bird in its branches. *Are you my death returned?*

Often she walked beneath it, letting her shade run into the oak's like ink. The wizened face in its trunk had stilled its tongue many lifetimes ago, but before that day the enchanter leaned heavily on its counsel. It was a night in Katherine's nineteenth year, as she ran her curious fingers again over its features—the wide mouth, the eyes obscured by ridges of brow, the nose a mossy furrow—that it shifted at last from its heavy sleep.

"Daughter," it said. "You are one like me."

Out of respect she snatched her fingers back, but felt no fear. "How so, grandfather?"

"You and I are Death-fed." Its bullfrog lips pursed. "My sap, your blood, are springs fed from Death's own river."

"What does it mean to be Death-fed?"

"It means peace will elude us, but have faith: it will be ours."

"I don't understand."

The oak tree sighed, a heavy, gusting breeze that blew green leaves into her hair. "I grow weary, my child. I would like, at last, to break my bond with the enchanter. To sleep without cease. Will you help me?"

"I know nothing of death," said the girl. "Only that I've escaped it."

The oak tree knew Katherine's living mind could not hold the glimmer of death too long in its waters, and chose his words carefully.

"There is no escape from Death, only delay. And you know more of dying than you remember. To help me, if you'll help me, you must seek out the witch from whom your father stole the words—those that allowed him to delay his death. Will you do this?"

Katherine looked at her father's window. The shade was drawn and its edges lit, not with the yellow of candlelight but the blue of magic being worked. She shivered to think of his scent when he drew too close. Clove and attar of roses, cloaking the sulfur-and-bitters tang of enchantment. His stippled jaw, the faint lines at his eyes that never deepened. When he'd found her bleeding in bed at the hand of his rival, in that beautiful house in that prosperous town, he'd spared her only the briefest look, and a handkerchief to press to her riven face.

"Yes, grandfather. I will."

Only one path led to the witch's cottage: the white road laid out on the sea when the moon was one day from full. The witch had married a Tide when she was young, and though the marriage didn't last, the Moon had allowed her to keep the cottage that was her wedding gift.

"Be unafraid," said the oak, "and you will find the path grows firm as stone beneath your feet. Long has the witch craved vengeance on your father. She will not hesitate to help you."

Armed with cloak and boots, a knife and her magic, Katherine left her father's lands to seek the witch and the words. She knew the sea lay past the edge of town, close if you had a horse and far if you didn't. On foot it took her four days to reach its shore. When she did, the new moon was rising, throwing filings of silver over the water.

Katherine sat on the sand watching moonlight break over the top of the sea. A coracle bobbed among the waves, the fisherman inside it casting his line into the salt. It went taut and, arms straining, he reeled in a piece of living light, wriggling like a worm as it came loose from the water. Again and again he cast his line, until he had a whole bucket of squirming silver. Then he poled to shore, climbing out to pull his vessel onto the sand.

He was broad but not tall. His hands were nimble and his dark skin scored with a crosshatch of scars, over his arms, neck, face, as if he himself had once been caught in a net. He didn't look at Katherine as he busied himself over his bucket.

She'd spoken to no one since her conference with the oak tree, sleeping in secret places and staying hidden when the sun was out. But her voice sprang free of her now.

"What do you use to catch moonlight?"

A smile spread like butter over his scarred face.

"Damselflies."

"What do you do with it?"

"Sell it to queens, to garnish their gowns."

He was lying, she'd learn later. He was teasing her. The moonlight could be fermented with honey to make wine. It could be mixed with milk in a bath to soothe old bones. If you added it to lamp oil, your lamps burned brighter, longer, and kept ghosts away. There were many uses for moonlight harvested from the Hinterland Sea.

Katherine learned them all, in the fisherman's cottage on the shore. When she married him, a month after they met, they drank moon wine to celebrate. And when her belly swelled with pregnancy, he rubbed moonlight in fish oil over her skin to soften it, and over her scar when it ticked with old pain.

Many months had come and gone by then. On the night before the Moon was at her fullest, Katherine always felt a pang, remembering her promise to the old oak. But what was one woman's lifetime next to the life of a tree? She would seek out the witch when she was old. She wouldn't forget the oak tree's wish.

Her labor began with a wrench and a rush of blood.

Katherine thought it would be easy, that her magic would smooth the birth along. Her husband had attended the births of animals both larger and smaller than she, and he thought they needed no midwife. Both of them were wrong.

The baby fought against the birthing. Katherine's body fought back, and it wasn't clear who would be the stronger. Katherine lost blood, more of it, too much. The voice was in her ears again, the voice she hadn't heard since the golden-haired enchanter laid his hands on her throat. *You are mine again,* Death whispered. *Here I am to catch you.*

In the end the baby was stronger than its mother, and Katherine's life gave out. No sooner had she touched down on Death's cold road than her body was reaching for a life that could bring her back. Her baby was close, so close, its fierce little body still nested inside her. Its life flowed like sap into Katherine. She was empty-eyed and still in her birthing bed, then alive again and screaming, as her husband slid his hands into her womb to pull the child free.

It slipped out gray-faced, with its parents' dark hair. Katherine and her fisherman wept over it, his face in her shoulder and their hands on the child. But the baby's thieved life was small and unsteady. Like all those newly born, it kept its toes dipped toward death. Katherine's body, weakened by blood loss and aflame with grieving and infection, extinguished it.

Her husband's life was stronger. With the will she could not control, gifted to her by her father's dreadful magic, she took it.

Twice-killed again, alive once more, Katherine lay on bloody sheets, the baby stiffening on her belly and her husband's body slumped over her shoulder.

A long time passed. She knew she must move but

could not. Her hands that could birth dark fruits, fleshy flowers, lay still. Her magic had died with her husband and child.

It took two days for another fisherman's wife to peek into their cottage, and a day after that for the midwife to reach them. It was a week before Katherine could sit up again. A week after that she was back on the road.

The journey was longer this time. Her body was damaged, though her life force was strong. She could hear her husband's heartbeat in her own, feel the ghostly twinges of injury that mimicked the flutter-kicks of the child she'd carried.

When she reached her father's land, it was not yet dark. She walked past the river and the stables and the silent oak. She walked through the enchanter's house, past startled servants, up to her father's workshop. She threw open his door.

He was waiting for her, raven on his shoulder.

"My daughter returns." His brow seemed untroubled but she knew him well, could read the rage in his tightening jaw.

"Did you fail to find your fortune?" he said. "Do you expect me to take you back? To continue your teaching? You've lost your beauty. You're dressed like a common fishwife. Your power is out of practice."

She didn't say a word. Lying beneath the corpses of her husband and child, she'd worked out the shape of her curse, and knew who'd given it to her.

She took a knife and ran it over her throat.

That hungry, life-seeking piece of her rushed at the enchanter. His color was high, his bones unbowed, he crackled with good health. But his life was a thing with no shadow: a hard, bright pebble, edgeless. Without the presence of death to cast it into relief, it could not be peeled away.

The house and its grounds hummed with people. Servants and children, the new wife the enchanter had taken in Katherine's absence, the baby he'd put in her belly. But they were too far away. Nearer to Katherine, and so imbued with magic by its master that its life shone with an unnatural light, was the raven.

Black-feathered, tarry-eyed, its years elongated by its covenant with the enchanter, the bird hopped on one foot. Katherine drank its life down.

All but the last little sip, which was tied to the bird with magic. Not as powerful as the spell that made Katherine unkillable, but nearly. That tiny piece of life folded itself up to the size of a seed, planting itself in the bird's smallest claw.

When Katherine woke, her front was heavy with blood and the bird clung to her shoulder. She felt their shared life tilting between them like the liquid in a spirit level. It wasn't enough.

Staggering to her feet, ignoring the enchanter, she ran from the room.

First they found a girl in a neat kerchief. A shriek

jerked out of her at the sight of Katherine, bleeding, weak, and wild, her arm weighed down by the raven.

"Go," Katherine whispered, and the bird obeyed. In a flash of feathers it stole the girl's life, its talons flexing and Katherine weeping with relief as their two bodies, hers and the raven's, were filled with it.

The enchanter's deathless daughter made her way through his house. By the end of it she glowed with stolen life, her skin plumped like a pastry and her hair blazing red for the first time since she was a girl. She held the bird against her breast like a baby as she returned to her father's room.

He'd heard the music of massacre and done nothing. All his long lifetimes cosseted by magic had made him weaker instead of strong. Katherine looked down at the fearsome enchanter who cowered before her.

"I spoke with Death when I was below. As my body tried to take your life, I petitioned him to help me, to kill you one way or another. And he told me something I wasn't wise enough to see."

"What—" The old enchanter—for he was, despite his youthful face, very, very old—swallowed dryly. "What did Death tell you?"

"That there are things worse than dying."

Fed on the strength of many, the girl and her raven descended on the enchanter and tore him into living pieces, as many pieces as years he'd had of ill-gotten life.

Ever after Katherine kept a piece of her father hanging at her belt—his left eye, rolling in its pouch, seeing nothing. Her bird she carried in a cage, loosing it when she felt the life in her faltering, for she had work to do: stealing the lives of arrogant men, and those who would tangle the threads of magic.

DEATH
AND THE
WOODWIFE

Beware the hollow-eyed men who make their living on the road; beware their riddles and the pretty things they sell.

In a valley kingdom where summer ruled, a good king lived with his wife. In the years of their marriage the queen gave birth to three daughters and four sons. A white rosebush was planted for every girl and a red for each boy, and the queen and her children spent many happy hours in the scented shade of their garden.

The years passed like turning pages and accrued like golden leaves, the princesses growing lovelier and the princes more handsome, until the day a wolf of the road came to their gates in the guise of a peddler. He stood at the courtyard's edge and sang up to the windows.

"Jewels for your daughters
Satins for your sons
Toys for your children
Me, I have none."

The seven royal siblings abandoned their lessons when they heard his song, running to the gates to let him in. In exchange for the rings on their fingers, he gave them brooches and scarves, carved cups and filigree thimbles. Soon they were running through the palace with their new trinkets, and the peddler was continuing on his wicked way, seven royal rings flashing from his hands.

The queen's youngest daughter died first, strangled by the peddler's necklace. Her eldest son was next, poisoned by the first swallow from his new willow cup. One by one, the princes and princesses fell, and by the time the king and queen heard of the coming of the peddler, it was too late. Their children were dead, and though they sent their fastest riders, they could not find the evil man.

The queen's joy died with her children. The last of her youth, the golden net of her laughter. She grew thinner, till the rings slid from her fingers and made a harsh music on the floor. She might, the king thought, have found solace in her garden. But as each child died, their rosebush died with them.

After her last child breathed his last breath, the queen took to her bed. She stayed there for seventeen days and nights, eating nothing, deaf to her husband's pleas. On the eighteenth morning she rose early and alone. On bare feet she walked through her garden, counting the places where her roses had been. At last she reached the place where an eighth rosebush would've grown, had she given birth to another child. From its plot rose a black sapling, narrow as a spike and dotted with green flowers. When she moved to pluck one, a hidden thorn pierced her skin. As she carried the bloom back to the palace, seven drops of blood fell to the earth behind her.

The next morning, seven more saplings had sprung up from the queen's blood. She moved among them, her grief finally eased. Each day they grew higher, until their branches met overhead and they made a thorn grove. The queen spent her days in the grove, walking beneath its waving green flowers, with a glove always covering the hand the thorn had bitten.

At first the king was grateful for his wife's change of heart. But her women whispered that her grief had only taken a darker turn. Her hours beneath the trees were spent conversing with her dead children, laughing with them, singing them lullabies. The day came when she refused to leave them, demanding her bed be set at the grove's heart.

The king could take no more. The thorn trees must be chopped down, he said, for the health of the queen. But, whether out of fear or sympathy, none of his men would follow the order. And so the king, older than he'd been, walked to the grove that night with an ax over his shoulder.

His queen waited for him in the dark, her own ax across her knees.

"For the love we have shared, for the love of our children, you'll turn back from here," she said.

One hand was on the ax, the other on her belly. And the king saw something that made the spit dry in his mouth. Though she hadn't shared his bed for many nights, the queen's body was swollen with pregnancy.

He wasn't angry, but afraid. Unshouldering his ax, he left his wife to her trees. He charged her women to keep her cool when they could, and warm when they must, and waited to see what she might birth in time.

When her labor began, the queen paced and howled among the thorns. Sometimes she shouted and sometimes she whispered, never to anyone the king could see. At the height of her pains she tugged off the glove she wore on her left hand. The midwife drew an astonished breath, but the king could muster no surprise. The fingers the queen had long concealed were not fingers. They were five thorn branches, their nails round green buds.

She labored long, and in laboring died, after giving birth to a tiny child whose skin was green in the light through the flowers. In her last moments, the queen ran her branching fingers over its head, blessing it in a language no one present knew. When the midwife carried the baby to the king, he saw that the tint of its skin was no effect of the light, but its true color.

The midwife feared for herself, and she feared, too, for the child. She worried the king might kill it. Sickly, alien thing though it was, she didn't want to see it dead. But when presented with the small green infant, its head fuzzed with dark hair and its ears whorled tight, the king took it into his arms. He spoke over it his own blessing.

But the midwife had heard the words the queen spoke to her baby, in that rolling, thorn-tipped tongue, and knew the king was too late. Whatever the child would do or become, it would unfold under the auspices of the queen's last blessing.

The queen was buried and mourned, her thorn grove chopped down, uprooted, and burned. The wet nurse claimed the child had writhed in her cradle as flame tore through the branches, but no one dared relate the tale to the king.

The child grew up beautiful and maybe even good, though no one could be certain—she rarely spoke a word. The king adored her and spoiled her in every way she allowed, having claimed her entirely as his own. He could only imagine what a stepmother might make of the silent, green-skinned princess, and he took no second wife. He kept his dead queen's memory close at hand, leaving her chamber exactly as it was when she was happy, before the peddler and the thorn grove. Her room was entered only by the maid who cleaned it, a flighty girl who didn't think to tell anyone of the single flower sitting in a glass by the queen's bed, still exhaling its strange perfume, as fresh as it was on the long ago day when she picked it. The maid only freshened its water and dipped her nose to its cup, looking at the queen's blood still clinging to the thorn below its petals.

The princess's skin never lost its odd hue, nor her fingers their unnerving narrowness. And while she was quiet, it wasn't because she was foolish, as some imagined. Nor dutiful. Nor good. She was quiet because she was waiting for something worth her attention. She didn't find it in the king who made her call him father, or the nurse who attended her without love. She found a trace of it, perhaps, in the painted face of the queen, but it was no use pining for the dead.

She might've spent the rest of her life looking for some unfindable thing in the corners of the palace. But when she turned sixteen the king roused himself long enough to command all the eligible men in his kingdom to attend three nights of dancing in his hall. He sensed his daughter was dissatisfied, and knew that finding a husband was her nearest means of trying on another life.

For three days and nights the palace filled up with princes and mothers and merchants and maidens, eldest brothers and seventh sons and girls who spun so fast on the ballroom floor you could see nothing of them but their hearts, laid out like bait for wolves.

In the first hours of the first night, the queen's leaf-skinned daughter watched from her jeweled chair as tales were made and unmade before her. She must've looked lovely sitting there, in a defiant white dress that made her skin glow greener. But the hours passed and the men in the room kept their distance. The night had nearly ended when the doors of the ballroom blew open with a crash, letting in a wind that made the candles gutter and the dancers draw close together, shivering.

In the doorway stood a man with the bearing of a king and the saturated eyes of an animal. His hair was black as an empty sky and his jacket was sewn with stars. They winked their tinny lights at the princess as he approached her, holding out his hand.

She was a girl who knew silence, who lived in and

loved it. But when his fingers folded over hers and he drew her into the dance, she understood what silence really was. This beautiful man with his predator's gaze was as cold and quiet as a forgotten grave. His presence ate up the voices and the music and the laughter, so she heard only the soft sighing of his breath.

When he let her go, half of the ballroom watched her with envy, the other half with fear. He bowed, kissed her fingertips, and took his leave.

The dancers spun on. Chilled through by the stranger's touch, the princess closed her eyes.

When she opened them, it was the second night of the ball. The dancing had begun. She was restless in sharp yellow satin, waiting on her chair, but no one dared approach her: word of her mysterious suitor had spread.

He arrived at last in a coat woven with the moon in all her aspects: infant, maiden, mother, warrior, seer. Again they danced in his miniature realm of quiet and cold. After a time the queen's daughter spoke into it.

"Who are you?"

The man smiled at her, the smile of a wolf.

"Do you see the way the young look at me?" he said. "With longing. With lust. I'm so far from them, they think I'll never catch up. Now look at your father, and your old nurse beside him—see how they watch me with fear? Ask them. They'll tell you who I am."

"I asked you," she said.

"I am the quiet," he told her. "I am the cold. I am the thing that comes after the end."

Then their dance was over. When he took his hands from her skin, the noise crashed in.

Before the third ball, the king came to his daughter's chambers.

"Have caution," he told her. "Beware of making a promise before you've made a choice."

She watched him in her mirror, eyes cool. "Beware of kings who speak in riddles," she said.

That night she wore black gossamer. Her skin against the dress was the delicate color of a slit cocoon. The man arrived just before night tipped into day. He'd worn stars and moons, and now the princess thought he might come in stitched suns. Instead he wore a coat that jittered with bones. Finger bones, jawbones, the clattering bones of the feet.

He pushed away the music and the whispers of those who watched them. Down a corridor of quiet he walked to her, tugging her to him as easily as he might snap a leaf off a branch. They danced again, but it was a formality. She couldn't hear the music.

"Who are you?" she asked again.

"A man who will wear a coat of knives on our wedding day," he said. "A crown of dreams, shoes of sand, and for our marriage bed a coffin."

Then he took her two small hands in his one and sealed his mouth to hers, taking the breath she'd sucked in when he gripped her. She supposed you could call it a kiss. When he slipped a ring onto her hand from his own smallest finger, the air around them shook with applause.

The queen's daughter held her head high. She let the stranger take her wrist and dipped her head at the king, cursing herself for not listening to his sage advice. When the ball ended she began planning her escape.

The princess had long felt it her right to visit her dead mother's bedchamber. Through patient eavesdropping she'd gathered the story of her birth and of the burning grove, but patience wasn't enough to gain entrance to the queen's locked rooms.

Now she devised a plan to steal the key from the maid who kept it. She had need of her mother's counsel, and though the woman was dead, perhaps she'd left something behind to guide her desperate daughter.

Taking the key was easy. Three glasses of punch to muddy the maid's head, and silver scissors to cut the chain the key was linked to. Before the sun had fully risen, the princess was letting herself into her mother's rooms.

There was a bed there, still lush with coverings. A cold fireplace clean as peeled wood, and a chest full of things the queen had brought from her parents' own palace, long ago, treasures wrought in glass and metal and wood. On a table lay a nosegay of white and red roses, dried brown and black. There was a looking glass and a trio of dolls with eerie faces and a footstool carved to look like a fat yellow dog.

The queen's daughter lingered by none of these. Her eye went to the flower canted carelessly in its cup.

Its bloom was the color, exactly, of her skin, its stem

the very shade of her hair. When she took it in her hand, it lit like a lantern. From its petals rose eight drifting ghosts: four handsome boys, three beautiful girls, and behind them a woman with long eyes and a sad smile. Speechless and shining, they beckoned at her. All moved their lips, but only the woman's words could be heard.

You are made of stronger stuff than he, the queen whispered to her daughter. *But your suitor has his tricks. If you wait until morning, it will be too late. Wear sturdy shoes and carry this flower. Go quickly now, and find your freedom in the woods.*

The princess left the palace by the kitchen door, setting off for the forest. By day she slept and by night she walked. The green flower lit her way, and if she wandered from the path her mother set her, its light would falter. Always it led her toward secret byways, to places where berries grew and water trickled, where moss made a soft bed. She walked for more nights than she could count, until she reached a clearing with a cottage at its heart. There, her mother's ghost appeared to her once more.

Rest in this place and do not leave it, she said. *Plant the flower at the clearing's edge, and it will keep you safe. It is dangerous to be a princess: forget your past. The one who seeks to marry you will forget you in time.* Then she kissed her daughter with a touch like a leaf falling over a stone grave marker and faded forever from sight.

When she was gone, the girl who must no longer be

a princess dug a hollow and planted the flower inside it. Then she knocked on the cottage door.

A widow lived there with her son. When they saw the girl in her dirty cloak, they took her in without question, giving her food and a place by their fire. They said nothing of her green skin or of the thorn tree, covered in flowers of the same hue, growing at the edge of their clearing. Though at first the girl was wary, she grew to appreciate their kindness.

The widow's son was a woodsman, handsome enough and willing to marry, but love of his old mother had kept him from seeking a wife. Now the two rejoiced in secret, because the woods had delivered a bride to their door. The girl was skittish, and loath to speak of her past, yet they knew they must win her in time.

"Be patient, my son," said the old woman. "See how the girl fears to poke even her nose outside our clearing? She's running from something very dark indeed. When her fears have faded, she will make you a happy wife."

The queen's daughter was no fool, but she was no woman of the world either, and did not perceive what the man and his mother were planning. When the woodsman took her hands in his a year after her arrival at his cottage, speaking words of love she could not return, she was stricken with fear. She appreciated her protectors, yet had no desire to become a woodwife.

"I cannot be your bride," she said numbly. A cloud passed over the man's expression, and she hastened on. "Unless you bring me what I desire."

His brow cleared. "Anything. What would you have of me?"

She thought quickly, searching for a thing this man could never find. "A treasure only a king could possess."

He bowed then to hide his smile, because he knew what to give her. The story of the green-skinned princess born seventeen years ago had spread far and wide, reaching even the woodsman and his mother. They'd guessed who the girl was long ago, and knew the flowering black tree was her own. A tree unlike any in the world, seen just once before, in the thorn grove on the king's own grounds. He'd bring her a flower from the tree, and with that gift claim her.

The woodsman waited until the girl and his mother were busy in the kitchen and approached the tree. He'd never come so close before. Its perfume was too heady, its branches unpleasant. Now it seemed to him that the tree was crying out in a chorus of voices he could almost hear, telling him to keep away.

He moved closer and the voices grew louder. Closer still, and the tree's shadows lit up with eight translucent bodies, hands out in supplication, drifting like smoke. Though he was terribly afraid, he was more determined to catch his bride. The woodsman closed his eyes and plunged his arm into its branches. A thorn caught his skin and tore it and still he reached, fingers closing around a green blossom and snapping it from its twig.

He shuddered in the sudden cold, as all the sounds of the woods went quiet. From the cottage came the crash of something falling, and he quaked, wondering what he'd done.

The cottage door opened. Through it came the girl he wished to make his wife, her arms before her, her eyes unseeing. She seemed not to hear him calling, nor to feel his hands as he attempted to hold her. She walked past the thorn tree and its broken protection, into the wild woods.

In her mind she was walking through the palace. It was the third night of the ball. When she pressed her hands to the trunk of a tree, she was opening the door of her room. When the tree opened to reveal a winding silver stair and she put one foot upon it, she was walking down into the king's ballroom, dressed in black gossamer. She could hear the sounds of the party below.

As the tree sealed shut behind her, two arms came around her in the dark.

"Together at last, my love," said the voice of the man of many coats. He stamped his foot and the silver stair split beneath them like an egg.

They fell for a long while and landed on the back of a vaporous horse. It carried them through trees carved from bright minerals, past lakes of pale fire. Her senses now restored, the girl knew they must be riding through the land of the dead.

The horse carried them to the doors of a jagged castle. They were led to a receiving room, where a great man sat in fearsome repose.

"Father," said her abductor. "I've brought home a bride."

Ah, the girl thought. *It is as he said. He is the quiet and the cold, the thing that comes after the end. Not Death, but his son.*

Death's son looked at her with pride, running his fingers over her throat, resting his thumb against her pulse. "Even in your kingdom, her heart beats true. She is a worthy wife to the prince of Death."

Death made no reply to his boasting. "A dozen of my son's brides have crossed into my lands, and none of them lived for long. Who are you, that your heart beats so strongly in this place?"

"I am a woodwife," she said, not daring to look at Death's son. "I am nobody."

"She is not—" Death's son began, but his father threw up a hand to silence him.

"Lies do not become a bride. Nor my daughter, whom you will be tomorrow, once you've wed."

"I am a woodwife," she repeated primly. "And married already."

Death twitched his lips, cut fine as ice. "Your husband has not followed you here, and the rules of the living no longer bind you. You will remarry tomorrow, but first I ask again: who are you?"

"I am a woodwife, who must now grieve the loss of my husband. I require three nights to mourn him before I can remarry."

"Far be it from me to dishonor the custom of wood-wives," Death said, his voice slow and dry as driftwood. "But time moves differently in the land of the dead. I will give you two nights, not three, before you must marry."

A translucent figure the color of cold tea stepped forward to take the girl to her room. Before she could follow, something batted at her ankle. She looked down to find a tortoiseshell cat puddling at her feet. Because it was the first living creature she'd seen in Death's kingdom, and because it looked at her with such clever eyes, she leaned down to greet it.

The cat spoke first. "They'll let you pick your chambers." It ran a tongue over its shoulder. "Be sure to choose the plainest room. No jewels, no hangings. Choose the room most fit for a woodwife." Then it padded out of sight.

Death's servant led the girl from room to room, each more wondrous than the last. She shook her head at each, until the irritated shade showed her to a crude, windowless chamber, empty but for a mattress, a fireplace, and a hook for a cloak.

"This one," the girl said. "This is where I'll stay."

"And may it bring you joy," growled the servant. Though there was no firewood, they coaxed from the ashes a spectral flame.

When she was alone, the girl knelt on the hard mattress, wondering why she'd listened to a cat. Then a scratching came at her door, and the creature let itself in. It warmed itself in front of the meager fire before speaking.

"Well done, but not yet done. You must listen to me

again, because I am your only friend here. You have not yet died, it's true, but even one such as you cannot withstand the land of Death forever. Your wedding dress will be your shroud if you don't make haste."

"One such as me?" the girl said.

The cat ignored her, grooming each of its limbs in turn. "If you marry that stupid boy, Death will be your father-in-law. Tomorrow you must ask him for an early wedding gift: a kiss. No matter what he offers in its place, accept only the kiss."

The girl promised to do so. The night she spent on her cold bed was long, and in the morning she rose exhausted. The servant fetched her, bringing her again before Death. He greeted her courteously, asked after her rest, and congratulated her that she still lived.

"Thank you, father," she said gravely. "I hope I'm not presumptuous in addressing you this way."

"A little, perhaps, my daughter, but I will make an exception."

"Then I must risk offense once more, and ask of you one thing. My wedding gift, early."

"A wedding gift," Death repeated in his slow red voice. "What do you wish of me?"

"Something small," she said. "Will you grant it?"

"I will. To make peace between us, and to show I do not take it lightly that my son stole you from your woodsman."

She curtseyed. "It's a small thing, as I say, in keeping with the custom of woodfolk. The night before a wedding, the groom's father must give his new daughter a kiss."

Death went still, so still the girl could feel it spreading. She was certain, for those moments, that all was unmoving in Death's realm. All but one small thing: in the room's farthest corner, tucked in shadow, the tail of a tortoiseshell cat.

"You may ask me for anything," Death said at last. "Anything but that. I have rooms full of jewels—take your pick. I have the life-lights of adventurers, enchantresses, queens. You may hold them in your hands and judge their weight. Bismuth caverns and groves of tourmaline. What do you desire?"

"I would not know what to do with any of that," she said, "being the wife of a woodsman. I only wish for your approval, father. And your kiss." Chastely, she offered her cheek.

When he spoke again, his voice had deepened from red to black. "I gave you my word, and you will have your kiss. But I will not descend to you."

It was harder than she thought it would be to climb the stairs to where Death sat in state, his long hands draped over the arms of his onyx throne. This close, she could see the swirl of his eyes, every color of weather. The charred wood shade of his skin and the bladed curves of his mouth. Standing at his feet she felt the life that ran through her like roots, and the places where it ran thinnest: her wrists and throat and temples. She turned her cheek to him like an animal turning its neck to the knife, and he pressed cold lips to her skin.

She tasted salt and metal. She smelled ashes and dust. The blood in her ears rose like a wave as her vision transformed.

She could see Death's hall truly now. Where before there were tapestries and bright lanterns, now there were peeling walls and guttering candles. Death's throne was in truth a tower of blackened bones, his rich red cloak tattered and eaten away. Only Death himself was unchanged.

"Happy marriage to you, daughter," he said softly. "Now you see my home, and yours, with clearer eyes. I hope you do not regret your choice of gift."

"Thank you, father," she managed. "On the contrary, it pleases me well."

His castle was a place of horrors now, of bone and decay. Only her room remained the same, cold and cramped and nearly empty, and she was glad of it.

She lay back on her cheerless bed. Almost as quickly she sat up again, looking at the hook on the wall. It was the only thing in the room that had changed: now she saw the truth of it. It was only pretending to be a hook; it was really a keyhole.

She waited for the cat. Soon its scratch came at the door, and it trotted in to stretch in front of her fire. The flames, she could now see, were the gray ghost of something that fretted and sighed, worrying itself into letting off a faint, sorrowful heat. The cat warmed its fur in front of the thing shamelessly.

"Good girl," it said. "But just one night remains, and now you must find the key. Your fiancé will invite you to dinner tonight, to gloat at his conquest. Say yes. Get him drunk, and make a wager. Tell him you can guess what he keeps in his innermost pocket. And if you guess right, make him forfeit to you the thing he wears around his neck."

And it laughed its hissing little laugh, leaning close to whisper the suitor's secret: what he kept in his inner pocket.

The girl agreed, and all was as the cat predicted. A knock came at her door, and a servant bade her come down to join her fiancé at dinner. She was taken to a decaying hall, where he sat at the head of an ancient table. In a coat of thorns, he watched her come.

"Good evening, my love," he said. "You are far too somber for a bride. You must eat and be merry."

The girl looked down the length of the table, and her eye was not fooled. Where delicate meats and golden pastries should be were all the flat black foods of the dead. She snubbed them, sitting beside her betrothed and lifting a glass filled with liquid thick as blood.

"Let us make merry then."

And she matched him, glass for glass, till he was drunk on Death's wine, made from the long purple grapes that grow from vineyards fertilized with battle-field blood. Her own wine she fed in secret to the cat, who nosed about her ankles below the table.

"I wonder how you live still," he mused. "I'd hoped you might. From the tales I heard of your birth, I knew you were something different."

He leaned closer, confiding. "My father is old-fashioned, and would have an heir of me. You must survive long enough to provide it. When you've done so you may die, or live, whichever I fancy. I think you'd better make me happy if you can."

The girl was not a queen's daughter for nothing. She lifted her chin and her glass and smiled through her hate. "You will find me an amusing companion, I think."

Her betrothed inclined his head slowly, moving with drunken care. "It amuses you to tell my father you are a woodwife. Perhaps we are not amused by the same things."

"A wager, then. Might that serve to entertain?"

"It depends." His voice dipped low, making a flirtatious hook that sought to catch her.

She lowered her own to match it. "I will bet you I can guess the thing you hide inside your clothes. In your innermost pocket."

His eyes sparked interest. "And if you win the bet, what must I give you?"

"Why, the thing you hold closest to your heart. The thing that hangs over it on a chain. I am to be your wife, after all."

He searched her face, and she kept it mild as milk. "And if you lose? What do I get?"

"A willing wife, of course." She held his gaze. "Who wants only to please you."

He set down his glass with a thump. "Done."

The girl leaned back and spoke as if to herself. "What does a man like you hide under his clothes? Something forgettable, to be sure. A thing no one would bother to seek."

His hand tightened around his wineglass as she went on. "You are the cold and the quiet, you told me once. The thing that comes *after* the end: after Death. I think you wish to be more than that. I think you want to be the one who does the impossible. The one who kills Death."

He struck her across the mouth, his breath gone thin and fast.

She stopped a drop of blood with her tongue. "A whistle," she said, her voice even. "In your innermost pocket you carry a child's whistle."

With shaking hands, Death's son reached below his jacket and pulled out a tarnished tin whistle.

Once in a century, the cat had told her, *exhausted by his labors, Death sleeps. Through the long night of his slumber, the sick sit up and smile. Knives steer clear of hearts, the drowning breathe in the waves. No one dies while Death lies sleeping, but he himself is vulnerable—only then can he be killed. He's protected in his sleep by a trio of hounds, but there's one thing that can draw them away: the music of his son's tin whistle.*

"What do you want from me?" Her betrothed's voice was strangled.

"Only what you promised. The thing that hangs over your heart."

He undid his shirt. Burning against his skin was the gold of a sharp-cut key, strung on a chain. He lifted it over his head and handed it to her. He did not follow her as she left the room, the cat following close behind.

It carried the whistle in its mouth. "It's not the time

for Death to die," it told the queen's daughter. "He needs a better heir first."

Back in her room, the girl hastened to slide the key into the lock, but the cat moved between her and the keyhole. It dropped the whistle from its mouth and sank back onto its haunches, lifting two paws to undo the fur of its chest. The fur fell away like a cloak, revealing beneath it a woman with green skin and hair black as branches.

"Do you know who I am?"

The girl looked at the woman, her hair and skin the very color of her own, but didn't dare guess.

The woman who had been the cat took the girl's hand in her own. "The queen was your mother, and I am, too. Death was too cruel in taking away all her children. I comforted her as best I could and gave her another daughter. When he took her from you in the birthing, I swore I would protect you. Death is my brother, and he comes for the lives of all women and men. But I, too, am Death: I carry away the lives of beasts, of insects, of plants and trees. I helped your mother make you, and I couldn't let my worthless nephew have you."

She kissed the girl's temple, on the opposite side from where Death had laid his lips. The hair above her kiss silvered over, and again the girl's vision changed. This time, all manner of beautiful sights were revealed to her: the hazy rime of spectral plants growing in the cracks of the walls, the delicate souls of dead flowers. A ghostly bird twittered in the corner; she could see the workings of its complicated heart.

The princess's own heart felt like a cup spilling over. Her other mother watched as she fit the key to the secret keyhole. Behind it was a landing, and another hidden stair. It went up, and it went down. She knew it would lead her, if she liked, back to the living forest. She could return to the palace, slip back into a life she knew.

But a wind blew up from below, from a place deeper even than Death's kingdom. It smelled of the dust of roads she wanted to walk and mysteries she'd like to consider. It smelled like no place she'd ever seen or imagined.

She set her course downward, leaving Death and his kingdom behind.

TAKE A JOURNEY INTO THE HINTERLAND . . .

PRAISE FOR *THE HAZEL WOOD*

'A DARKLY BRILLIANT STORY'
Wall Street Journal (Best Book of the Year)

'A CAPTIVATING DEBUT'
The New York Times Book Review

'A BEGUILING MIX OF CONTEMPORARY
THRILLER AND DARK FANTASY, coupled
with stylish, sharp prose, makes this a
dangerously addictive debut'
Bookseller

'ALBERT IS A NATURAL STORYTELLER
who writes with the confidence of an old hand'
Daily Telegraph

'THIS BOOK WILL BE YOUR NEXT OBSESSION.
Welcome to the Hazel Wood, where bad luck is a living
thing, princesses are doomed and every page contains a
wondrously terrible adventure – it's not safe inside these
pages, but once you enter, you may never want to leave'
Stephanie Garber, bestselling author of *Caraval*

'*THE HAZEL WOOD* IS THOROUGHLY,
CREEPILY CAPTIVATING, WITH SURPRISES I
NEVER SAW COMING. Such a beautifully written
inversion of the classic fairy-tale-inspired story'
Kristin Cashore, bestselling author of The Graceling Realm series

READ THE ORIGINAL
BESTSELLING NOVEL . . .

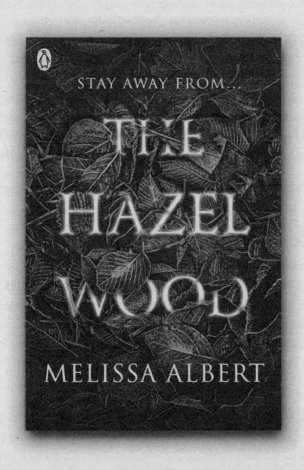

PRAISE FOR *THE NIGHT COUNTRY*

'A LUSH AND ENCHANTING TALE. Albert effortlessly draws on a wide range of literary references and builds a world where magic really does emerge from pages and where books are not just figurative but literal doors. Dreamy and disturbing in equal measure, it's the perfect antidote to a grey winter's day'
Irish Times

'A SINISTER JEWEL OF A NOVEL, like splitting a pomegranate and finding the inside filled with blood and rubies, every sentence of this book thrilled and chilled me to the bone'
Melinda Salisbury, bestselling author of *The Sin Eater's Daughter*

'ALBERT'S LEGION OF FANS WILL RELISH HER RETURN to the bloody, terrifying, seductive world of her debut and the inventive brilliance of her storytelling'
Guardian

'MELISSA ALBERT DEFTLY WEAVES HER MAGIC ONCE AGAIN between our world and the fairy tale realm of the Hinterland. *The Night Country* is a new modern classic filled with wondrous delights and daring forays into the dark. Not to be missed!'
Kim Liggett, author of *The Grace Year*

'*THE NIGHT COUNTRY* IS SO DELICIOUSLY CREEPY – the kind of puzzle box nightmare you have to see through to the end. One of the most unputdownable books I've read in a long time'
Emily X. R. Pan, author of *The Astonishing Color of After*

FOLLOW THE
TRAIL . . .

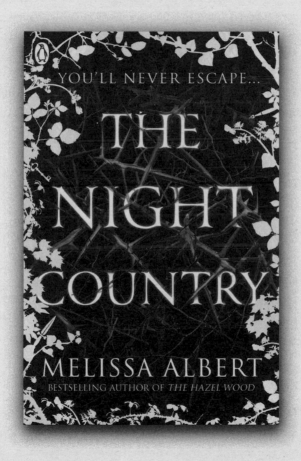